S0-DQZ-908

THE
TWILIGHT
ASSIGNMENT

A NOVEL

LYMAN L. MARFELL

Copyright © 2022 Lyman L. Marfell
All rights reserved
First Edition

PAGE PUBLISHING
Conneaut Lake, PA

First originally published by Page Publishing 2022

ISBN 978-1-6624-6829-2 (pbk)
ISBN 978-1-6624-6830-8 (digital)

Printed in the United States of America

CONTENTS

ACKNOWLEDGMENTS

My most sincere and heartfelt appreciation to Dr. *Lynn Brann* for her worthwhile and patient efforts to make sense of the rough draft of this book. It is a far-better literary effort on my part due to her excellent proofreading and copyreading ability, as well as her continuing encouragement.

Hearty thanks also go out to the *Wheatland Writer's Group* for suffering through my reading of each chapter of this book at every meeting and their muted but helpful critiques.

MAIN CHARACTERS

Edmund Rambar—retired CIA operative
Loretta Scaradelli—fiancée then wife of Rambar
Larry—friend and former coworker at CIA
Nigel Brown—supervisory MI6 agent
Dorris Brown—wife of Nigel Brown
Wanda Wendover—former actor
Kirk Hanrahan—MI6 agent
Viktor Borenko—Russian agent
Captain Demetriopoulos—freighter commander
Patric nephew of Rambar
Obadiah S. E. Pulcher—mortician

CHAPTER 1

The Offer

As usual, several older locals had gathered for their morning coffee and bullshit session at the only diner in the remote Wyoming town. Another man, also elderly but a newcomer, walked out of the building as the "geezers" eyed him with some degree of interest. He had been a topic of conversation before

"There's somethin' odd about that guy, just cain't put my finger on it," Ernie offered, addressing no one in particular.

"Well, yeah. He seems like a reg'lar guy, but he sure keeps to himself. How long's he been here now? Maybe six or seven months?"

"Let's see. He bought the old Carson place in September of last year, wasn't it?"

"Nobody knows much about him at all," Virgil added. "I heard that he was in some kind of a government *witness protection* er somethin' like that," murmured Fred Olson.

"Some more coffee here, Connie?" Five cups were raised to receive it from the chubby smiling middle-aged waitress as she brought the steaming pot over to their table.

Later, around twilight, a nondescript green car pulled into the driveway of the former Carson house the diner "geezers" had talked about that morning. The rural-style mailbox was now labeled E. RAMBAR.

It was easy to tell the old house had been given some recent attention. The trim work had been painted a bright tan to accent the brown shingled exterior, and young saplings had been planted in the front lawn.

The driver ended the call on his cell phone, got out, and walked briskly up to the front door while surveying the surrounding area. He appeared to be late middle age, average appearance, and had on a conservative suit and tie.

Pushing the doorbell, he stood to the side, not directly in front of the doorway. The door opened partly, and Edmund Rambar began smiling.

"Well, for God's sakes, Larry, I haven't seen you in one hell of a long time! What brings you up to this neck of the woods?"

"Hi, Ed. I can't say I was just passing by, not to a godforsaken place like this. Can I come in?"

"Sure, get in here, you old rascal. How long has it been anyway? Y'want some coffee or maybe something stronger?"

"Well, a drink would hit the spot. What do you have? Damn, it must be at least twelve years or so by now. It's great to see you again, old buddy."

Ed walked, slowly with a slight limp, over to a cabinet and removed a half-full bottle of Drambuie. Grabbing two glasses, he returned to his former associate.

"Okay, now what brings you all the way up here? It can't be good news because it never was whenever I saw you in the old days. As you just might happen to know, I'm retired, in fact, longtime retired."

"Yeah, yeah, I know, but in this business, you're never really retired until you die, remember?"

At that moment, a large rust-colored dog walked into the room, wagging his tail and gave one friendly *woof.*

"This is Hunter, my friend and companion. Had him about four years now. You have a dog, Larry?"

"No, I'm still on the job and traveling a lot. It would be kind of hard to have a pet, even a cat. Nobody wants to take care of 'em when you're off somewhere."

"So I'm pretty sure you didn't just stop by for a drink and talk about old times. You've gotta want something, or the agency does, right?"

Larry and Ed had known each other and worked together off and on for way too many years to try bullshitting each other.

"Yup, you're on to me, old buddy. I'm up here because the agency told me to come, not that it isn't great seeing you again. You *do* look older, and I'm pretty damned sure that I do too, don't I?"

"C'mon, Larry, get to it. What the devil does our *beloved* agency want from an old codger like me now? I gave them more than thirty years of my life. Can't they just leave me in peace? Probably I don't have too many years left anyway. Got one bad knee, and I've slowed down a hell a lot since I was on the job, y'know."

"Okay, here's the deal, and I think you might just like it. It's nothing too hard, but you're one of very few people who could pull it off and probably the only one who might be available. Your Anglophile background plus the fact that you're so damned anti-technology and computer illiterate make you exactly the right man for this. Besides, you were a real chameleon in the old days. You could change your appearance just like that and confuse the hell out of the bad guys.

"We need someone who wouldn't raise much suspicion if he were, say, doing something clandestine. Perhaps someone of the British aristocracy and particularly someone older, even slightly disabled, as I notice that you are kind of are.

"In this super-sophisticated age, no one would even consider using a courier to carry intelligence. You're about as low-tech as they come, therefore, a perfect choice."

"Sadly, I can't deny that there are a lot of miles on this old carcass, so why should I even consider taking on *any* kind of an assignment? I'm retired and damned happy to be retired."

"Ed, you know it's not my doing, but the agency never leaves anything to chance. We've checked your bank account and credit cards. You're not exactly flush with money right now after helping your kids out with buying a house and—"

"Ah, Larry, you wouldn't be trying to strong-arm me now, would you?"

"Hell no, Ed, we're not threatening to kidnap your grandkids or whatever, but we think this might be an opportunity to help us out and give you a good financial cushion at the same time. You can just tell us no, and I'll go away and try to find another operative, but none of them will be as good as you, old buddy."

"Flattery will get you everywhere, huh? Well, tell me something about what you want me to do and what's in it for me—financially."

"Okay. Somewhere in the agency, there's a well-placed *mole* that we haven't been able to flush out, besides all the computer hackers. That being a proven fact, we can't trust our normal channels to get some vital intelligence across the pond to MI6, except to utilize an undercover courier. We've put all our intelligence eggs in one electronic basket, and it's been a bad mistake. It must be someone with an impeccable record, well experienced, and is always fully alert. Your *cover* would be that you are an elderly member of the aristocracy returning home after visiting relatives in Canada."

"Well, it sounds *just* wonderful. How much is this adventure going to be worth by our penny-pinching bean counters? Are all expenses being taken care of, and can I have full control of how I'd do it from start to finish?"

"We know you like doing it *your way* and you are always successful. The agency said okay. However, you decide to play it, subject only to our general scenario. We're talking $300,000 for this assignment, and it's just a quick onetime round trip. You'll have a really fine wardrobe to keep too, another added incentive."

"Wow, this has to be one hell of a big deal for Uncle Sugar to put out that kind of bucks."

"It's the biggest, even discussed at the White House, and it's in the daily summary provided to the president. Let me fill in the specifics. First, we fly you up to Toronto. You'll have all the documents including a British passport supporting your *cover* story. Then you catch a British Airways flight to Heathrow and check into your reserved room at a hotel in Mayfair, something consistent with your noble persona.

"You rest up for a day and then call an encrypted number we'll give to you for the information drop. Our British counterparts at

MI6 will be fully briefed that important information is coming over but not how or by whom, in case there might be a *mole* in their organization, perhaps even in contact with whoever ours might be."

"Okay, I'm interested in how this would work. You said something about me playing an older aristocrat, right? Now how would you want me to carry the intelligence, surely not in a briefcase handcuffed to my wrist or some other hokey-spy-movie crap?"

"That's something I can only tell you once you agree to take on the assignment. No other specifics until you say yes."

"I'll need a little time to think it over. After all, I am seventy-eight years old, and to go out on something like this could offer physical challenges that I'm not capable of meeting anymore, if all doesn't go as smoothly as you suggest. Let me sleep on it overnight, Larry. We can have breakfast and talk about it in the morning."

CHAPTER 2

Accepting the Assignment

Ed was making breakfast when Hunter barked that someone was arriving, and an electronic sensor signaled the same. Larry walked up to the house, petting the dog as it approached him.

"Morning, Larry," Ed called from the kitchen. "How did you sleep? That motel is definitely not the Ritz."

"Well, it wasn't bad, considering everything. It was quiet, the sheets were clean, and no snakes in the bed. Smells like you've got some food cooking, and I am kinda hungry."

"If you can stand my cooking, there's some pancakes on the stove. How about a cup of coffee?"

"Sure, anything's fine, but it's not like when we had wives to take care of us, is it?"

"I've been giving it a lot of thought since we talked yesterday, and it seems to me that it's damned risky to entrust something of vital importance to some doddering old man. So we both know that there'd be a serious backup just in case—probably a couple of dependable shadows, right?"

"You haven't lost a beat, Ed. Yup, at least two agents will be your shadows and on your tail at all times until you get it delivered. Of course, it's also for your personal safety too, you know."

"If I happen to lose them, how will the agency pick up my trail again and not leave me hanging?"

"I know how you hate anything complicated. Our electronics geeks have it programmed so you'll only need to touch one number

8 to contact both agents at one time unless you need to call someone else, then it works like any other cell phone."

"How about when I need to call MI6 to arrange the drop?"

"Again, only one number, which will be 7, think 007 to remember. It will connect with the right guy there, and you'll have a code word or phrase to use."

"Then it'll be the same if I need to contact the shadows, right?"

"Yeah, again code words on both ends, you and them, but push number 8."

"Considering everything, I did a financial calculation last night, and I won't take on this gig for less than $400,000. Take it or leave it."

"Believe it or not, the chief thought that would be the case, so your price will work. In fact, and I shouldn't tell you this but we're old friends, the agency would have gone up to half a million, if need be."

"Larry, I'm not greedy. Just figured out what I'd need to be comfortable. Here's how I want it to be paid. As you know, sometimes government agencies kind of forget about payment, so I want it in advance, $200,000 in a certified check. And the other $200,000 in cold hard cash, right in my hand before I take one step forward."

"Hm, that might complicate things somewhat. Your price is okay, but I'll have to get my butt down to Denver real fast to get it all together, and then I'm sure you'll want to put it safely away too. This takes valuable time before we can get this underway."

"C'mon, I know how the agency does things, and it can be done fast if they're motivated enough, which it seems they are. As you mentioned before, I'll need that proper wardrobe of clothes befitting a noble lord. So let me give you all my measurements."

"Wow, Ed, like always, you do plan way ahead. Complete outfits will ready for you to pick up at a custom men's store, Savile Row, of course. Some will be used clothing to give you an authentic appearance. I understand that most of the upscale shops are doing refurbishing of their own brands.

"You'll have a Harrods charge card for incidentals and lots of cash. They'll be provided at the airport in Denver along with the passports, a British one and probably an Indian as well or whatever country you prefer, okay? Now the big question is, will you do it?"

"It looks like this will be my *last hurrah*. Yeah, I'll do it—if everything is how I want it including the money up front. It does strike me as odd that I'll be needing a lot of clothes for just such a short gig."

"Well, the agency thinks of everything too. If there should be any delay, you'll be covered. The last thing you want to worry about is having clean clothes."

"I can begin all this happiness the day after tomorrow, on Tuesday, if that works out for the agency and they can get everything together by then. Now I'm dying of curiosity, how will I carry the intelligence?"

"In your mouth, Ed."

"What?" Ed shot him an incredulous look. "In my mouth? Maybe you should hire my dog, Hunter, instead."

"Sure, we've checked, and you have semipermanent dentures that snap into place, right? We managed to get hold of your dental records—don't ask me how—and a duplicate of your upper plate is being made right now. It will contain a computer chip, kind of like a thumb drive, which I'm sure you don't know what the hell that is. It'll be embedded in the plastic or whatever they're made of now.

"Then when you arrive in London, you give that plate to your contact over there. Take your own denture along with you to wear again once you've deposited the *loaded one* with your contact."

"Okay, got it so far. Now about the identification code for both MI6 and my shadows over there."

"When you push number 7 on your cell phone, a voice at MI6 will say 'This is Christopher' to which you will reply 'This is Rancourt.' If you want to speak with either of your shadows, push number 8. Same code words, but if there should be any doubt whatsoever on either end, you can add 'This is AC4YN' to which the other party will say 'Lhasa, Tibet.'

"We chose that phrase because of your great interest in things Tibetan, and if there is still any doubt, you can ask, 'Who ran that radio station?' If your legitimate contacts reply with 'Reginald Fox,' then you're good to go. Only MI6 and the two shadows have been briefed on that last part.

"There's one more thing too. You'll have an emergency number in case something should go wrong at the immigration in Canada, the UK, or coming back home to the States. We'll give you a business card to carry, and it'll say 'The Executive Office of the President' along with the number. Just keep it handy and present it to any official who might question you. Have them dial that number, and *voilà* you're home free. You probably wouldn't remember the number to call in a stressful situation, hence the card."

Pulling out an imaginary sword from a scabbard, Larry went through a ritual. "I dub thee Edmund, Lord Chesterton-Rancourt of Northumberland. You won't be listed in Debrett's peerage, of course, but the 'bad guys' don't know who's listed anyway. They're creating life peerages all the time, and that publication only comes out occasionally, so there is no way of checking your authenticity."

"Oh yes, what's the name of the tailor shop where I pick up my fancy clothes?"

"It's called *The Huntsman*, which should be easy for you to remember with your doggie named Hunter, right?"

CHAPTER 3

En Route

Early the next afternoon, Larry pulled up in front of Edmund's house in rural Wyoming armed with an attaché case containing currency, a certified check, and various documents including an Indian diplomatic passport and a worn-looking British one.

"What kind of goodies have you got for me, old buddy?" Ed joked as he met Larry at the door. Hunter wasn't sure if he knew this man, so he investigated by putting his nose in Larry's crotch in the time-honored canine manner. Satisfied, he began wagging his bushy tail vigorously.

"Pretty much everything you ordered, Ed. Your tickets and we got the passports earlier than I'd figured, so they're here too and lots of UK money. Oh yeah, and the business card I told you about and your Harrods charge card."

"Okay, I'm going to head over to the bank and do some errands. I think it might be better for me to drive down to the airport alone tomorrow and not ride down there with you. That meet with your approval?"

"Sure, Ed, however you want to do it. Your flight leaves at 4:00 p.m., so you have plenty of time to get there. I'll head back to Denver now and see you tomorrow."

Shortly after Larry took off, Ed called his neighbor and friend Loretta about taking care of Hunter. "I need to visit some relatives in Canada, near Toronto, for a few days. Shouldn't be gone much more than a week. Will you look after Hunter for me? Thanks. I'll bring him over tonight if that's okay."

Then he drove over to the bank in nearby Douglas to deposit the certified check and pick up a few items for the trip. Back at home, he located his old strongbox, put the $200,000 cash inside, and took it downstairs to hide in the stone cellar. Then he gathered up Hunter along with his favorite chew toys and walked over to Loretta's place. "Now you be a good boy, and I'll be back soon," he said as he hugged his favorite companion.

Returning home, he sat down with a glass of Drambuie on the rocks and looked through the passports and supporting documents that Larry brought him.

"Ah, even personal calling cards for Lord Chesterton-Rancourt, a nice touch."

Deciding to stay overnight at a hotel near the airport, Edmund awoke refreshed and as fully alert as he used to be when on assignment.

His cell phone rang and the voice said, "This is Christopher."

He responded with "This is Rancourt."

"Authenticate."

Thinking for a moment, Ed replied, "AC4YN," to which he heard back a "Lhasa, Tibet."

"Good, Ed, this is Larry. Just wanted to check that we were *in cahoots* and that you were in Denver."

"Yup, I came down last night, so I'm definitely here. Have you had breakfast yet? I'm getting ready to go to the place downstairs. Know which hotel I'm at? Oh, silly me, you have a GPS fix on my phone, haven't you? That also means you knew I was down here."

"You've got me, Ed. The agency leaves nothing to chance. I'll meet you there in about fifteen minutes. Order me some coffee and whatever you're having."

Larry arrived in exactly fifteen minutes, and while eating, they made last minute small talk.

"Here's something to get you through security real fast. These stick-on letters *P A* look like a monogram, but put them on the side corner of your carry-on luggage. It stands for *Priority Access*, just be sure the agent there sees it."

Being the nontechnically minded man that he is, Edmund had wanted hard-copy tickets to present at the check-in counter and for the London connection in Toronto.

"Is there anything else you can think of, Ed, or did we cover everything? If not, you can ask me when I meet you at the airport lounge at 1:00 p.m. I'll have two escorts with me because that's where we outfit you with your new choppers. From the moment you get to Denver International Airport, there will be shadows with you until you drop off the intelligence at MI6."

"No, I think we're *copacetic*, old pal, so I'll see you at the airport."

* * *

Larry was waiting for Ed to show up at the lounge. He had just picked up a package containing the loaded dentures. At 1:08 p.m., he checked his watch wondering what had kept Ed. The female escort glanced anxiously toward the door then at Larry.

Then Ed walked in hurriedly, carrying a Denver newspaper but using a cane that could conveniently fold if necessary. "Sorry to keep you waiting, but I stopped at the newsstand. Don't get a paper up where I live, so this is a treat for me."

"Just glad you made it here. Let's go over to a corner where we won't be disturbed to make the switch. If we all went to the men's room together, it would look really strange, especially since one of us is female."

After unwrapping the package, he handed Ed the plastic case containing the dentures.

"Let's hope to God it fits right, or we're in deep doo-doo," Larry said nervously as Ed put it in. It clicked into place as he smiled and felt it with his tongue.

"Bit of a sticky wicket if it hadn't," Ed commented, going into character. He put the container into his case, closed it, and shook hands with Larry.

"Do you have your disguise kit with you, Ed?"

"Like American Express, I never leave home without it, at least when on assignment. Changing one's appearance is quite simple, really. As you know, people doing personal surveillance mostly focus on only two or three characteristics of their subject. So I try to change the most obvious things, just enough to throw them off and create doubt that they're looking at the same individual."

"I know you can pull it off. I saw you do it many times when we worked together. I learned a lot from you back then," Larry replied with genuine admiration.

"Well, you know the old saying, Larry. 'Keep your friends close, but keep your enemies closer, right?'"

"By the way, haven't you forgotten one thing, Ed? How about your new cell phone? You might possibly need it some time."

"Oh crap. I'd forget my own head if it weren't hooked on. Thanks, Larry."

It was 1:35 p.m., and followed by the two escorts who were to accompany him on the flights to the UK, Ed made his way to the gate. Then after taking two pain pills, he started reading his newspaper, waiting for the flight to Toronto to begin loading.

Once aboard, he settled back into his window seat and relaxed. *God, I'm already tired*, he thought. *And I still have to get to London.*

CHAPTER 4

In Character

The flight from Toronto had been rough with considerable turbulence, and Ed was happy to be back on solid ground, or at least on solid airport floor. He barely slept at all and lamented how much more exhausting flying eastbound was than going west.

Fully in character mentally, Ed proceeded up to the immigration desk.

"Long flight was it, sir?"

"Yes, beastly long and bumpy. I shall be quite glad to be home again, but I must stop off in London for a few things first."

Stamping the ersatz lord's passport, the agent handed it back, commenting, "You may want to consider getting a new one sometime soon."

"Oh, really? Why is that?"

"You see, sir, the expiration date is less than a year distant, and it appears that you've been using it quite a bit."

"Well, eh, yes, rather. Thank you for being kind enough to remind me," he said as he limped off. *These damned bags seem heavier than they used to be*, he thought tiredly. In the main concourse, he stopped to find a water fountain. Glancing around, he noticed a pair of Middle Eastern-looking men looking everywhere with determination. They seemed to be paying particular attention to older white men and approached a few of them.

One came up to him and asked, "Do pardon me, sir, but are you an American by any chance?"

"Good heavens, no, and I am not accustomed to being accosted in an airport," Rambar replied with obvious irritation.

"Oh, please do excuse me, sir, I am looking for someone whom I must meet here."

He carefully watched the man depart and approach another older man a short distance away. Thinking to himself, *Hm, I wonder if the mole at CIA or NSA got hold of my profile information?* The Middle Eastern guy glanced back at him a couple of times, perhaps unsure if he had already found the right man. He didn't come back though and continued questioning other elderly travelers.

On a hunch, Rambar decided to buy an umbrella as he put the folding cane away in his suitcase. He entered a shop and told the clerk, "I wish to purchase a brolly, something in a plain color, preferably dark."

As he emerged from the shop, a sharp pain came from his right knee joint. *I better try to sit down for a few minutes. Maybe a cup of coffee will help*, he thought and limped over to a refreshment stand nearby.

"I should like a white coffee with two lumps," he told the counter attendant, a large surly Black woman who had no interest in being there.

"The suga' over on de little tables where you gonna sit, mon. That be two pounds fifty."

"Ah, this is actually good. I can watch those men while I rest." At that moment, he noticed a second similar-looking man approach the first one. Their brief conversation seemed almost frantic as they continued looking around nervously.

"I tell you, Ahmed, this is like looking for a man dressed in white, attending the Hajj. We have nearly nothing to go with—an older American man with a bad limp. Have you received further information, anything?"

The other guy shook his head negatively.

Rambar wished he could hear them although he realized immediately that they wouldn't be speaking in English. *I wonder how much they know about me or even if that's what they're doing in the first place?*

Finishing his coffee, the knee pain somewhat subsided, Rambar stood and tested his walking ability.

As he left the refreshment stand, the two men looked over his way and decided to follow at a distance. Trying not to limp, he walked briskly as possible to a nearby staircase. Hurrying down, he abruptly turned to the left side and ducked while waiting to be sure the two men were really after him.

Soon, he heard them coming down rapidly, jabbering loudly in Arabic or Farsi. Except for them, the stairs were unoccupied. As the first one touched the sixth step from the bottom, Rambar thrusted his umbrella low through the balustrade, tripping him.

He fell, landing on the floor below, cursing, while his companion rushed down to help him. Rambar hurried away and spotted a men's room. "Time for a costume change," he joked to himself.

Pressing button 8 on his cell phone, he gratefully heard a professional sounding voice say, "This is Christopher."

"This is Rancourt."

"Authenticate."

"AC4YN."

"Lhasa, Tibet."

"Are your people in place yet as my escorts?"

"Yes, we are, and we have you in sight as we speak. You may communicate with us on this same number at any time. We can hear you clearly."

"Are you both nearby?" Rambar asked somewhat anxiously. They answered affirmatively.

"Thank goodness. Come down to the men's quickly. Two Middle Eastern men are following me. One may be injured, but I suspect they won't give up easily. Try to delay them if they want to enter that room. I will be making a change of appearance, but it will take me several minutes. Then when I come out, I will appear to be Indian."

Tired but charged up, Rambar opened his suitcase in a stall. He slapped a decal sticker onto his case. It read "Visit Exotic India" and showed a brightly colored picture of the Taj Mahal. Then he pulled out a cap common to most Indian traveler and turned up his coat collar, making it look like a Nehru jacket. Last, he donned an Indian-style cloth shoe covers.

Leaving the stall, he approached the mirror and wash basins. Opening a small jar, he quickly dabbed some light-brown skin color onto his face and the back of his hands. "Hm, not bad considering…" Eight minutes had elapsed as he walked out of the men's room, trying to avoid limping.

One of his pursuers had arrived but was being engaged in a furious conversation with an apparently very pregnant woman in her late twenties.

"Please help me, sir. That man molested me," as she pointed in a general way, causing the Middle Eastern pursuer to turn away from Rambar's direction.

The second man, obviously hurting and hobbling along with great difficulty, arrived and glanced at the first one while looking around carefully. Rambar's male shadow bumped into him, making it seem accidental, causing him to fall clumsily to the terrazzo floor.

"Oh, I'm frightfully sorry, old boy. Are you injured?" the shadow asked solicitously while helping the man up. This attempt was not successful, and both tumbled back again with the shadow's left knee landing on the injured man's arm, momentarily pinning him down.

"Again, I'm so very sorry. Terribly clumsy, I'm afraid."

Rambar knew what was happening and signaled discreetly to his shadows as he hurriedly departed. *God, I'm exhausted. I've got to get over to the hotel and die for a few hours*, he thought. Still, despite his tiredness, something kept nagging at him. He turned to watch his pursuers, saw them look around frantically and then take a seat while assessing the loss of their prey.

Well, I could rest for a while before leaving. Ah, there's a seat near them. Looking nonchalant and trying not to limp, he ambled over and took a seat three places away. Evoking only slight interest from the two men, he put down his suitcase making sure the "Visit India" sticker faced them. While bending over, he appeared to accidentally drop the Indian diplomatic passport out of his jacket. It landed front side up next to his bag, noticed by one of the men.

"Oh dear, I find myself getting more clumsy all the time," he exclaimed loudly, in feigned anger at himself, using his best Indian voice. After retrieving it, he took out his cell phone, pretending to call someone.

"Hello, this is Jawaharlal. Yes, yes, I do understand, but this is more than silly. If you do not stop this nonsense, Rajeev, when I return to India, I will take you to Rajanpur and throw you into the Ganges. You will not like this, but it will purify you and get such foolishness out of your head."

Overhearing the loud conversation, both men shook their heads in frustration, thinking they had lost whom they had been pursuing. Without a glance at Rambar, they left, still desperately hoping to locate their intended prey. He watched them depart with satisfaction and then went out to hail a taxi.

In the taxi, he changed his appearance back into British, much to the amusement of the driver. After checking in at The Dorchester hotel, he dropped onto the bed in his room, number 714, removing only his topcoat and jacket. He fell to sleep almost immediately.

CHAPTER 5

Meets His Shadows and His Enemies

Awakening somewhat refreshed the next morning, although painfully aware of his seventy-eight years, Rambar stretched and mumbled to himself, "God, I hate getting up and going through my morning miseries every day."

After getting dressed and somewhat put together, he decided to call his shadows, pressing 8 on the phone.

It answered, "This is Christopher."

"Rancourt here. Meet me for breakfast downstairs in about twenty minutes. We need to discuss our strategy."

Looking like a young couple, the two saw Rambar and greeted him as a long-lost friend. "Your Lordship, how long has it been? You look as chipper as ever." They're speaking enthusiastically.

Always in character, he said quietly, "I felt it might be most beneficial to determine just how well informed our *friends* might be at this point." Both nodded in agreement.

"We doubt if they have managed to trace you this far, sir, although they may have done since your hotel reservations were made in the States."

"I do feel that they are quite certain they have the right old man spotted, and they tangled with you both at Heathrow. My goodness, you don't look at all pregnant this morning, my dear," Rambar joked. "Obviously, an overnight abortion. Do tell me what to call you both."

"Yes, sir. My name is Helen, and this is Rupert."

"My thought is that I shall continue proceeding as planned and see if they decide that I don't seem to fit their profile. There may also be other pursuers working with them."

"Do try to contact MI6 as soon as possible, sir, and get your information transferred. We realize that it is most important to get any pursuers off the trail and give you more freedom to make the contact. Fortunately, they don't seem to have the sophistication of Russians or the Chinese," Helen commented thoughtfully.

After finishing breakfast, they're prepared to leave but then noticed a pair of Middle Eastern men walking into the hotel restaurant. One of whom was someone they had not seen before, probably a replacement for the guy who was injured by his fall at the airport. One, whom Rambar had encountered before, spotted him and informed his new partner. Helen and Rupert went in a separate direction but remained close. Rambar went outside and took a taxi to the Huntsman men's shop in Savile Row.

As soon as he departed, one of the two men asked the doorman, "Pardon me, but do you know who that gentleman is?" pointing to the taxi.

"Argh, I think 'e's one of those blinkin' aristocrats, always thinkin' they're better than us workin' folks."

After about forty minutes, Rambar emerged from the shop, looking very much the English lord, wearing completely new business attire with proper hat and cane. Having the rest of his clothes and accessories delivered to The Dorchester, he looked around with casual interest. Then hailing a taxi, he ordered the driver to take him to Harrods in Knightsbridge and still in sight of his two shadows.

Leaving that department store, Rambar returned to his hotel room and pressed number 7 on his cell phone. It rang and a male voice said, "This is Christopher."

"Rancourt here."

"Authenticate."

"AC4YN," and the reply stated, "Lhasa, Tibet," then "Further authentication required."

"Who ran that radio station?"

"Reginald Fox," though not having to provide so much authentication before.

"That is correct, Lord Rancourt. You are requested to appear at Marble Arch this afternoon at precisely 2:30 p.m. Wear a black handkerchief in your jacket breast pocket, and when a woman dressed in black approaches, pull it out and accidentally let it fall to the ground.

"She will smile and greet you with 'The weather is somewhat better in Monte Carlo.' This code phrase is unknown to anyone except me, the woman, and now you. If she does not tell you this exact sentence and the proper codes, break contact and depart immediately."

At 2:15 p.m., Rambar got out of a taxi and walked the two blocks toward Marble Arch. He waited there looking for a woman in black apparel. An old lady approached with a small dog on its leash and stopped to let it urinate. Then she went on past him and crossed the street. It was now 2:40 p.m., and no one else appeared.

At 3:00 p.m., Rambar decided to call MI6 again to find out why there was no contact. "This is Christopher."

"Rancourt here. No one met me. Do you know what happened?"

"Actually, I don't."

At that moment, a thin woman wearing a burka appeared and walked directly over to Rambar. "This is Christopher."

He immediately sensed this was not the true contact and surmised that she spoke English badly. He said, "This is Ramekin."

"You authenticate please?" she asked.

"Acetylene," Rambar replied.

She continued, "Los Angeles."

Must break contact quickly, he thought. Out of the corner of his eye, Rambar saw two men running toward them from nearly a block away. The woman pulled out a gun, telling him, "Give me what you are carrying."

"Whatever do you mean, my good woman?" he replied innocently while clumsily knocking the weapon out of her right hand with his umbrella. It fell onto the pavement and discharged. The bullet flew across Dunraven Street, striking the balustrade of a townhouse. Her two cohorts ran up to them but were followed immediately by Rambar's shadows who pounced on them.

A fierce scuffle ensued as the burka-clad woman attempted to flee. Despite his arthritic pain, Rambar grabbed her as she struggled to get away. *Feisty bitch, isn't she?* he thought. Relying on his former training from decades ago, he managed to put a choke hold on her and she collapsed momentarily. The covering on her face fell away, revealing a dark-haired younger-looking *man* with a moustache.

Rambar saw him and gasped. "My god, I didn't know I could still do that."

Two police constables in a panda car, a block away, heard the shot and raced to them. They arrived with "What have we here?"

Rambar replied first, "I am Edmund, Lord Chesterton-Rancourt. We have a few fine specimens for you to arrest."

His two protectors showed the proper identification, still holding the suspects at gunpoint.

One explained, "This is an MI6 operation" and provided a contact number. "We'll be along shortly to file charges and provide statements."

The two bobbies cuffed the suspects and called for a transport vehicle.

"Good work you two. Don't think I could have managed on my own," Rambar joked but with genuine appreciation. They all grinned at each other and chuckled. "Now I must ring up MI6 myself." He pushed number 7 on his cell phone.

The voice answered with "This is Christopher."

"Rancourt here, AC4YN."

The reply was "Lhasa, Tibet."

Without prompting, he said, "Reginald Fox."

"Yes, Lord Rancourt, your associates there just informed me about the imposters. I really didn't expect they knew that much or could quickly stage such a ruse. Still, they have no idea of what it really is."

"Would it be possible for me to merely take a taxi over there to your office and give it to you directly?"

"Unfortunately, that would not be possible for several reasons, which I'm not even privy to myself. You see, we are considering using you for something on your return trip. It is best if we keep you unidentified as much as possible. Now that we have derailed, at least temporarily, their little intercept plan, they will need to get different players to stage another attempt.

"We are quite certain the three now in custody will be screaming bloody murder and claiming diplomatic immunity or something. Actually, that will be good and will get them out of the UK quickly. Perhaps it may give us sufficient time to complete this operation."

"That does come as a bit of a relief." Rambar sighed. "I find that I'm just too old to be tackling the villains these days. It takes longer for the body to heal."

"Very good, Rancourt. You choose where you would like to pass along the intelligence. Let your associates there, Helen and Rupert, know, and they can give it to us via their channels, hopefully undetected. Is that all right?"

Rambar concurred.

"It is vital that we relieve you of the information most expeditiously. So do choose a drop point quickly. Oh yes, I am called Nigel, and with your permission, I shall refer to you as Edmund going forward."

CHAPTER 6

Intelligence Is Transferred

"There's a restaurant on Greek Street that I'm going to use for the drop but will not disclose the name or location to MI6 until a half hour before our meeting," Rambar told his shadows. "Also, my MI6 contact thought it would better if I convey any information of that sort to him via you two. I did not indicate it to him, but I disagree. Before we arrive at that location, I shall call him myself."

The male shadow frowned almost imperceptibly, not looking at his counterpart, who nodded in agreement.

"Yes, the fewer people who know, the better," she said.

When they arrived, Rambar called MI6.

"This is Christopher," Nigel stated.

"Yes, Rancourt here. AC4YN."

"Lhasa, Tibet," Nigel responded. "Where are we to meet?"

"At a place on Greek Street called *The Four Hussars* in thirty minutes. Can your people get there that soon?"

"Yes, Edmund. However, that will be a tight time frame. I've decided to come along myself with a few escorts. What is your location at this time?"

Rambar crinkled up some paper close to his cell phone. "I... think...our...connec...is...bad." More crinkling of paper and scraping it across the phone. "Will...mee...t...yo...u...there."

Nigel knew it was an old standard trick in clandestine operations to avoid being pinned down. Rambar's phone did not have a

GPS although one of his bodyguard's did. *Clever old devil, not taking any chances*, Nigel thought. *Good for him.*

When they arrived, Rupert excused himself and went to the men's room. Thirty-two minutes later, Nigel entered the place accompanied by two heavily built young men. He looked around the small establishment and noticed an elderly couple sitting near the windows. A table near the back held Rambar and his people. A youngish, apparently gay, couple walked in, sat at a nearby table, and chatted audibly.

"I'm Nigel, and these are two of my coworkers. You are undoubtedly Edmund, correct?"

"I'm sorry. Don't believe that I am acquainted with you... Nigel, is it?"

Again, Nigel knew the stall. "I am referred to sometimes by my last name. It is Christopher, originally from Lhasa, Tibet."

"Ah yes, AC4YN. I had a friend there named Reginald Fox who operated the radio station."

Then Nigel followed up with "The weather is somewhat better in Monte Carlo, isn't it?"

Satisfied that both men were actually who they were supposed to be, Rambar took a bite of meat and began choking. He hurried toward the men's room, motioning for Nigel to follow him. He did and began slapping Rambar on his back to dislodge the food.

Inside and alone with Nigel, Rambar quickly removed the denture and placed it into a small plastic bag he had. Then coughing convincingly a couple of times, he handed it over and exited. The MI6 man stayed behind to urinate.

"God, I'm glad to be done with that," Rambar sighed to himself as he sat down to continue eating. "Damn, I forgot to put my own denture in." Quietly, he managed to slip it in place.

In a few moments, Nigel appeared and signaled his men, and they all abruptly departed. The waiter looked surprised as they left.

Outside, still in sight from the window, Rambar and the shadows heard tires squealing as a car veered toward Nigel and his men. Stopping just short, three men jumped out and attacked them, grabbing Nigel and forcing him into the car. It sped off.

"Oh, oh, they've got him!" one of the shadows cried out.

Immediately Rambar's two shadows ran outside, followed by the gay-looking couple, then himself, limping badly.

Inside the vehicle, Nigel grabbed one of his abductors by the throat and managed to toss the plastic bag containing the dentures out of the car.

It dropped on the roadway at Rupert's feet. He scooped it up quickly, furtively looking around to see if he had been seen.

Always aware of everything, Rambar approached him. "Ah, thank you, Rupert," as he snatched the bag firmly. *Quite impressive of Nigel*, Rambar thought. *But God that was too close, they almost had it.*

Helen phoned in the situation and told her contact to immediately put out an "all sectors lookout" for the fleeing car. She had been very alert and saw the license number as it left, which had also been observed by several of the thirty plus omnipresent security cameras all around London.

Reluctantly, Rambar placed the denture back into his mouth after quickly taking out his own. "Damn it, here we go again," he grumbled to himself. Then he wondered if he should call MI6 again and chance speaking with someone not in the loop. Followed at a distance by Helen and Rupert, he considered his options.

After resting on a bench and taking two pain pills, he decided to call the emergency number on the card Larry had given him.

"This is Rambar in London. Do you require authentication?"

"No, this is a secure line."

Then he continued. "I've run into a problem. My MI6 contact has been abducted, and I'm not sure if I dare contacting that number blindly."

"Stand by for now, Rambar. We'll get back with you."

He was exhausted and returned to his hotel room. Resting uneasily, he lay back on the bed, waiting for the agency to call him. An hour went by, then two. Finally, his phone rang.

"This is Christopher. Good news. Your MI6 contact has been rescued and his abductors arrested. You will be able to contact him again directly in the morning, your time." The phone call ended.

CHAPTER 7

Testing His Escorts

At 9:00 a.m., Rambar called MI6 and identified using the codes.

"Ah, good to talk with you again, Edmund," Nigel greeted him. "I had *a bit of a go* there for a short time, but all's well now. Perhaps we can get back to our main objective."

"I should most certainly wish to do so, Nigel. If we could simply learn who our elusive mole is, then we should be able to complete this operation."

"To begin with, I feel it would be advisable to even change your bodyguards. Admittedly, it would be unlikely there is any problem with them, having been thoroughly vetted. But trying to eliminate any remote possibility, let's have a go at setting up another rendez-vous tomorrow."

"Actually, I've grown rather accustomed to having Helen and Rupert as my shadows. Still, in my mind, everyone is a suspect until proven otherwise, so I'd like to use them for our next endeavor and see if it proves successful...or not."

"Of course, Edmund, it is very much yourself in the line of fire. So let us do this. We will have one of our people meet with you for the transfer at 8:00 a.m. along The Embankment, immediately by the statue of Queen Boudica. Our man will be properly attired, someone of your social position, and holding a book titled *Our Man in Havana*, an appropriate name, I should think."

"I'm going to try a little test on my watchdogs. First, I will give some of the details to Rupert but with a few inaccurate points. Then I'll do the same with Helen."

"It's definitely worth a go, Edmund. We haven't had much luck thus far. If one or the other does pass along the information you give to them, it will likely flush out our mole. Good idea, old boy. Needless to tell you, I shall be the only one here who has any knowledge of what you're up to. Good show."

A bit later, Rambar, always known to his shadows as Lord Chesterton-Rancourt, asked them to meet with him in his room at The Dorchester.

"Helen, Rupert, I've just spoken with MI6, and we're having another go at it tomorrow morning. The transfer will take place near the statue of Queen Boudica along The Embankment. It will be with a young man in blue jeans, striped jacket, and wearing an old bowler hat. He will ask me if I can spare a quid for a drink."

They both nodded with keen interest though his male shadow frowned slightly.

"Oh, Rupert, would you mind going down to the gift shop and getting me some throat lozenges? A package of the Fisherman's Friend. I've been having a scratchy throat today. Thank you so much."

"Helen, would you have a drink while we're waiting? Then you can join us when you return, Rupert. Perhaps it may even be a toast to the successful conclusion of our little adventure."

Rambar poured two glasses of brandy, giving one to Helen. "We should wait to toast until Rupert comes back. I didn't mention it to him, but the young man is an Asian and carries a portable oxygen device. Keep that part to yourself, please."

God, I can't believe it's only been four days since I was talking with Larry about this caper, he thought to himself.

* * *

A gentle rain had begun falling the next morning as a light breeze swept off the Thames River. Rambar began walking toward the Queen Boudica statue. About fifty meters from the rendezvous point, Rupert spotted a young man running along the path. His appearance roughly matched the description. Although he perceived the jogger to be Lord Rancourt's contact, he was wrong. It was only an innocent person who happened to be on the scene. Seeing this as his only chance before the transfer could be made, Rupert suddenly closed in behind Rambar, grabbing him around the neck, choking him.

"Give me your denture, Lord Rancourt! Nothing personal, but I'll kill you if you don't!"

Losing breath rapidly, Rambar attempted to throw Rupert over his back. However, his strength failed, and Rupert held him fiercely. Helen rapidly closed in on them.

"Rupert, what the hell are you doing? Release him!" she shouted.

"Get back, Helen, or I'll do him in. I mean it! Don't think I won't."

"Are you totally mad, Rupert? Do you know what you're doing?"

"I know precisely what I'm doing, Helen. Now back away, or I'll shoot you!" he shouted back while fumbling for his weapon.

Rambar reached weakly for his denture and pulled it out, trying to hand it over his shoulder before collapsing. As he slumped down, Helen saw that Rupert had his weapon in hand and aimed toward her. She pulled out her gun and fired. It struck Rupert in the neck, causing him to release his hostage. Blood spurted out as he fell to the pavement.

"Oh god, Rupert. No...no. Why did you make me do that?" She cried and dropped down beside him, her tears mixing with the raindrops. She sobbed uncontrollably. "Rupert, why...why?"

Still gasping for his breath, Rambar fell to his knees, retrieving the fallen denture, then tried to console Helen. She was shaking violently as he wrapped his overcoat around her. He looked at Rupert, whose eyes met his. "Whatever made you do this, Rupert?"

"For...for Allah...Islam." He went limp as his eyes closed slowly. He was gone.

They struggle to stand up, Rambar still holding his coat around Helen, as they both shiver in the rain.

"You saved me, dear Helen. He nearly killed me. Try not to grieve for him. Sometimes those we love are those who do us harm." He was crying now too, shaking his head at the futility of it all.

Trying to gather his composure, he told her, "We must stop this, my dear. There's nothing more ridiculous than some damned old man crying like a silly school girl."

She looked back at him gratefully as they both sniff a few more times.

"I know, sir, but we worked together for such a long time and…I thought…we were good friends or even more."

"Now, Helen, I must apologize. I gave you some false information when I described my contact at The Embankment. Just a test to learn who the *mole* was. We didn't know it was Rupert at that time. Very sorry."

A panda car wailed in the distance. Someone had heard the shot and called the police. Meanwhile, waiting by the Queen Boudica statue, Rambar's actual contact also heard the disturbance and the shot. He decided that something had gone terribly wrong and quickly departed and then called his superior at MI6.

CHAPTER 8

Rendezvous with Nigel

That morning, after a night of fitful sleep, a disheveled Rambar roused himself. He had fallen into bed, having taken off only his coat and jacket. "God, what's next?" he mumbled, aching all over and stumbling toward the shower. Feeling slightly revived, he called Nigel at MI6.

The now-familiar voice said, "This is Christopher."

"Rambar here. AC4YN."

"It's all right, Edmund. A secure line, remember? Terrible business about Rupert, but I think we've found our mole. We've been putting it all together now. At the airport, he had to show you, and us, that he was a trustworthy fellow. Besides, it was a much too public location to try forcing you to give him anything. He really didn't learn just exactly where or how you were secreting the information at that time. Actually, he only figured it out when I threw the denture out of the kidnappers' car when we left the restaurant on Greek Street."

"Of course, that makes sense, Nigel. But why didn't he try to do something at Marble Arch? He could have let the assailants have a go at me right there, couldn't he?"

"Well, you fouled up the works for them when you were able to knock the gun out of the hand of the man in the burka. When the weapon went off, it alerted the police. He heard their siren start up and their tires screeching, then he realized that Helen was running toward the scene with weapon drawn. At that point, there was no choice. He had to continue playing his part."

"Why did he try it on his own at The Embankment? Didn't he have his cohorts standing by to help him? After all, he had plenty of time to notify them after I fed him the false description of my supposed contact, the young runner."

"Yes, we did wonder about that ourselves. Somehow, there was a foul up, and his people may not have arrived in time to be in place, or he may have accidentally given them the wrong time or location. We'll perhaps never know for certain. It really doesn't matter much now."

"That does relieve my mind considerably. Now perhaps we can finally transfer the information to you. This was a great deal more than I'd bargained for."

"Quite. However, we've hit another bit of a snag."

"What do you mean *a snag*, Nigel? Don't tell me there's another *mole* at your office."

"Unfortunately, there does seem to be. Our people tell me that it is likely a Russian operative. They are pursuing that angle most rapidly. The Iranians are basically amateurs at this game so far, but the Russians or the Chinese are a different matter."

"Oh, that's really quite lovely, isn't it, Nigel, and then there's still the fact that my agency, back across the pond, has at least one *mole* still there too."

"Our most immediate concern, of course, is relieving you of the information. So I'm going to meet with you myself to get it and then have you come over here so we can discuss something else. My plan is to have you don one of your famous disguises, rendezvous at some location, then transport you back here. Does that sound all right?"

"Yes, definitely. I'll have on something different this time. Wearing the Indian garb might already be compromised though I doubt it. This will be an Orthodox man, a Hasidim. I shall be just inside the lobby of my hotel at 2:00 p.m. and wait for you to arrive."

"You should be easy to recognize, Edmund. I will be in a regular taxi except that it will have a yellow scarf caught in the passenger door as though some woman had forgotten it."

CHAPTER 9

Rambar Offered Vacation

At exactly 2:00 p.m., a taxi pulled into the porte cochere of The Dorchester hotel. Rambar immediately saw the piece of yellow scarf hanging out the bottom of its door. Wearing his new black suit from Huntington's, he walked briskly toward the cab. Inside he saw the familiar face of Nigel and two other men. As he advanced, Nigel noticed that he somehow looked both shorter and portly.

"Excellent disguise, even down to the beard and side curls. I could swear that Edmund is a Jewish rabbi or something," he mused. "Hello, Edmund. Let me introduce two of my associates. This is Jack Durkin, and he will take over as Rupert's replacement. Along with Helen, they will be your shadow team. This second gentleman is Harry, but he will only be with us back to the office. Now before anything else goes wrong, do let me have our denture. Oh, did you bring your own to replace it, Edmund?"

"Yes, I actually did remember to bring it along," he said as he produced the chip-embedded upper plate and placed it in a small plastic bag. Then from a second one, he took out his own denture and put it in his mouth, giving a toothy smile. "I can't express how very relieved I am to have that over with. Mazel tov."

* * *

Arriving at MI6 headquarters, they exited the taxi after going through several garage doors of unrelated but adjoining buildings.

41

Nigel conducted a tour of the agency, then they settled into his office on the top floor near the holy domain of "C," the head of it all.

"Would you like a drink, Edmund?"

"Yes, that would be delightful," he said as he watched Nigel fill two cordial glasses with Drambuie. Rambar smiled at Nigel for knowing his favorite drink.

"You did a splendid job for both our countries, and Her Majesty's government is most grateful. Therefore, we would like to reward you with a short holiday along the Mediterranean before you return home, all expenses covered, of course."

"How very wonderful, Nigel, and I gratefully accept. Now just who do I have to assassinate to receive this offer?" Edmund replied, joking skeptically. Knowing from many years of experience that there is, indeed, no free lunch.

"Ah yes, Edmund. There is just one minor thing. We have been passing along information to Interpol in France as part of our reciprocal agreement. As with so many intelligence agencies, the French have also been plagued with a mole in their operation.

"So recently we have been relaying intelligence through the police in Monaco, then they deliver it directly to Paris or some other city. It is our belief that there are no leaks within the Monegasque agency. Therefore, any subversive within the Interpol operation would be unlikely to think much worthwhile information would come from them."

"As reciprocity for my holiday in, presumably, Monte Carlo, I would be acting as a courier for MI6, correct?"

"Precisely, Edmund. We have been using our own people until recently, but they are well known and easy targets. When you came along, being an unknown, we felt this a perfect opportunity to thwart their efforts for a while. Are you interested in helping us?"

"I've not been to Monaco before, and it does hold some interest for me to see it once. But I'm tired and really would prefer to go home now. Still, I'm thinking about doing it, provided there are no complications involved. However, considering how much Her Majesty's government is offering to pay for this little messenger service, there has to be more involved."

"Actually, it should be quite straightforward. Also, we would offer you an honorary knighthood, if Her Majesty approves, which we are quite certain she would do. While it's a great honor, in itself, there is also a modest stipend as well, something in the range of fifty thousand pounds."

"Let me understand this correctly. All I have to do is carry something down there and give it to someone with whom MI6 will put me in touch. In return, your agency will give me an all-expense paid holiday, a knighthood, and a sizeable bonus, right?"

"That's about all of it, Edmund. The information will be packaged as a gift and, if opened, will appear to be only a small book. A reservation will be made for you as Lord Chesterton-Rancourt, keeping you in character. The Hôtel Hermitage on Charles II Avenue is only a short stroll over to the Monte Carlo police station. There, you will contact Inspector Lucien Gerard and give the parcel to him. After the delivery, you will be completely free to enjoy your well-deserved holiday in a style befitting a member of the English aristocracy."

"Let me give a call to a neighbor of mine back home who's caring for my dog, as well as watching my house. If all is well, then I'll agree to do it for you."

From MI6 headquarters, he placed a call on his secure phone. "Hello, Loretta. I have to go to London for a few days, a family matter. Would you mind watching Hunter a bit longer? I should be back home in about a week at the most. Oh, thank you, thank you very much. I'll bring you something nice from London. I think that's it for now. Yes, unfortunately, my knee has been acting up, but I have my pain medication with me, so I'll survive. Bye for now, and thanks again. You're an angel."

Edmund ended the call and faced Nigel. "Everything's back home. When would you like me to leave?"

"We can set up the airline and hotel reservations by tomorrow. Helen and Jack will be with you at all times. She will act as your personal secretary. Jack will shadow you at a discreet distance but is always within immediate help if needed. Now get out of your Jewish garb before some rabid Islamist gets hold of you. Oh, and stay away from any Sharia area. Unfortunately, we have some of them right here in London."

Rambar thanked him and departed in the MI6 taxi.

CHAPTER 10

Heading to Monaco

Deciding to order a nice gift for Loretta, he stopped by Harrods Food Hall and had them prepare and ship a basket of edible goodies. Although still somewhat shaken up, Helen helped him pick out the gift for his neighbor. She wanted to continue on as Lord Rancourt's bodyguard and accompany him down to Monte Carlo.

Needing to stretch their legs, they left Harrods and walked a few blocks along Brompton Road in Knightsbridge with Jack trailing along. Rambar was still in his Orthodox garb, planning to change once back at The Dorchester. Suddenly they were set upon by three Muslim men who hurled insults at the "filthy Jew."

Thinking quickly as always, Rambar stopped, turning toward them. "Stop this nonsense at once, you fools. I'm an actor over at the East End, in costume for a play. I'm no more Jewish than you men are. Look," he said as he pulled off his beard and side curls. "Now do you still think I'm a Jew?"

Helen had her weapon ready inside her coat pocket in case, and Jack hurried in closer to them. The three men looked embarrassed then quickly walked away, shaking their heads. "Now shall we continue our walk, Helen?"

* * *

The next afternoon, armed with the small package and wallets full of euros, Rambar and Helen boarded the flight to Nice, France.

Jack was also on the flight but appeared to be not acquainted with them.

Monaco is too short of land area for an airport, but it offers an excellent heliport on reclaimed land from the Mediterranean. When the party arrived in the south of France, they boarded a Heli Air Monaco chopper. Soon they were settled into their hotel rooms at the Hermitage, and Rambar was eager to get the package over to Inspector Gerard.

Helen joined him in his suite and called the police station. "Hallo, *vous parle Anglais, n'est pas?*" she asked tentatively.

"Of course, madame. How is it that we may assist you?" the polite desk officer asked.

"*Merci*. I would like to speak with Inspector Gerard, please."

She was immediately connected with him, and she handed the phone over to Rambar.

The inspector answered, "Hello, this is Inspector Gerard. With whom do I have the pleasure of speaking?"

"I am Lord Chesterton-Rancourt and have a small package for you from your *uncle* Nigel, in London."

"Ah yes, of course. How is my dear uncle?" Gerard replied cordially, immediately picking up the code. "He called and told me you would be in Monaco very soon. When can I meet with you?"

"I'm settled in at the Hermitage and could walk over to your office within a few minutes."

"That would be splendid, sir. I presume that you have someone accompanying you?"

* * *

It had begun raining steadily, somewhat unusual for Monaco, except that the weather was turning into autumn. As they passed a large fountain on the boulevard, Rambar slipped and fell hard onto the pavement, his umbrella flying away. He yelled out, "Damn it."

Helen tried to help him onto his feet, but he cautioned her, "Do be careful, please. I fear that I've broken my arm."

Jack saw them and hurried closer but acted as a helpful bystander.

"Let me get you over to a hospital quickly, sir. I'll hail a taxi," Helen told him.

"No, Helen. We must get this package over to Inspector Gerard first."

"Oh dear, if we must," she said as Rambar slowly and carefully stood up. With Helen supporting him, they made their way over to the police station.

The building was a fussy-looking one-story Beaux Arts structure on the east side of the boulevard, fitting perfectly into the elegance that is Monte Carlo. Once inside the door, a young gendarme hurried over to assist Helen with Rambar.

"Inspector Gerard is expecting us," Rambar said weakly, as Helen nodded.

He appeared from his office and realized that something was not right with his visitor. "What has happened? You are Lord Rancourt, am I correct?"

"Yes, I am," Rambar replied as he pulled the package out of his inner coat pocket. "I seemed to have injured myself. Slipped on the wet pavement just near the fountain."

"It is all right now, monsieur. I will have a car take you to the Princess Grace Hospital immediately. Thank you so very much for bringing this," he said as he accepted the small parcel.

* * *

At the hospital, an elderly doctor informed Rambar that he had suffered a hairline crack to his upper right arm, along with minor bruising. With his arm in a sling, they left the facility, riding back to the hotel in the provided police car.

Unruffled and always in lordly character, "Perhaps we can begin our Côte d'Azur holiday now without further mishaps," Rambar told Helen.

Smiling back, she asked what he might enjoy doing in Monaco. Jack Durkin had joined them for dinner. With the package delivered, there was little need to keep a distance between them. Nevertheless,

Jack came over to their table acting as if they were casual friends from the UK.

"I would be most interested in the Exotic Gardens above the city. Then the museum in the palace, changing of the guard, and the cave with neolithic drawings. That should be quite sufficient for one day's touring, don't you think?"

"Yes, Lord Rancourt, that would be really enjoyable. Would you perhaps like to join us, Mr. Durkin?"

"I would be delighted. However, I do have some business to attend to in the morning. Could we meet for lunch and then do some sightseeing?" Jack asked.

"Yes, there are so very many things not to be missed here, I'm told. How long will you be in Monaco?" Rancourt asked.

"Not really certain yet," Jack replied.

Although observed with only casual interest by the many resident foreign spooks, Helen and Rambar enjoyed visiting some areas of interest. Once, they even inadvertently stepped into France briefly due to the completely open border demarcated by only white paving stones and a marker at the east end of Monaco.

The ratio of police, both uniformed and in plain clothes, is higher in Monaco than in any other country. This is because of the great percentage of extremely wealthy residents and visitors, many of whom are casino patrons. Largely owing to this, Rambar and his bodyguards could move around freely without undue caution.

"It is my understanding that there is a good quality perfume factory here in Monaco. I would like to purchase something special for a dear lady I know," Rambar told Helen. "Perhaps we might stop by and see just what scents they offer."

Taking a taxi, they arrived at the shop located up on Le Rocher, not far from the prince's palace.

CHAPTER 11

A Bad Feeling

By now, more than a week had elapsed since Rambar arrived in London. For the first time, he felt somewhat relaxed, confident that his escorts were friendlies, not double agents. His basic trust was well-founded. Coupled with his nearly infallible instincts, he knew if someone was friend or foe.

On their third day of sightseeing, they were contacted by Inspector Gerard. He asked if Lord Rancourt would mind taking a letter back to Nigel at MI6 when they depart the principality. Talking over any security concerns with Helen and Jack, Rambar decided to repay the kindness he'd been shown when his arm was injured.

About ready to return to London, he stopped in to see Inspector Gerard. As he was handed the thick sealed letter, it came with a most serious caution.

"This information is even more important than the parcel you brought me a few days ago. We now believe that there is a Russian agent out to either obtain it or somehow destroy it before you reach London. Be very careful, Lord Rancourt."

Reservations for all three had been made on Air Deladier, leaving from Nice to Gatwick Airport near London. As they left Monaco by taxi, Rambar had a bad feeling about it. Whatever he was carrying apparently had much importance to the Russians who, until now, had not appeared on the scene.

What puzzles me is how the Ruskies found out about me and what I'm carrying back to MI6, he thought as they drove westward along the coast. *There has to be a leak somewhere in the chain*, he deducted. *But where?*

Approaching the airport, Rambar told the driver, "Take us to the railway station instead."

Surprised by the sudden change of plans, Jack and Helen looked at him, wondering what he had in mind.

"Do you not like flying, Lord Rancourt?" she asked.

"I've decided that a change might be good right now," he explained. "If there is someone, or perhaps more, awaiting us at the airport or on the plane, then we must disappoint them by not making an appearance. We can take the Train à Grande Vitesse up to Paris, then the connecting one through the Chunnel all the way to London. Admittedly it may take a bit longer, but I'll feel safer."

Arriving at the station, they bought one-way tickets and settled back for a snack before the train departed in forty minutes. Meanwhile, at the Côte d'Azur Airport, a confused pair of Russian agents looked around nervously for an elderly English aristocrat with a limp and an injured arm, probably accompanied by a younger woman.

At Victoria Station, Rambar phoned Nigel, informing him they had returned and that he carried a sealed letter for MI6. A taxi from the agency was immediately sent out to retrieve them.

In Nigel's office, Rambar mildly complained, "This whole business has gotten somewhat more complicated than what I'd bargained for. First Iranians, now the Russians. However, before I return home, I'm taking a bit of time to visit my nephew down in Peckham. In truth, he's a cousin but has affectionately called me Uncle Edmund since he was a little boy."

"I dread telling you this, Edmund, but it was most fortunate you decided to return here by train. You see, the Air Deladier flight you were booked on crashed and everyone was killed. The French aviation people believe there was an explosion on board."

"How terrible. I had a strange feeling about it, almost a premonition. Don't know why, but it kept nagging at me before I decided on the train. Once I did, everything seemed all right again."

"The reason that you are being so well paid for this recent little venture down to Monaco," Nigel went on, "is that there was some degree of danger involved. We thought that an individual with your experience and, well, cleverness would be preferable than sending down one of our known agents."

"Somewhat understandable. However, it would have been nice to know that the Russians were tailing me," Rambar said quietly, handing the letter to Nigel.

"Do you feel that it would be wise to visit your nephew, considering your mission over here, Edmund?"

"He has no idea of what I did for the government, and this could be my last opportunity to see him. After all, I'm not getting any younger. I'll invent some excuse as to why I'm over here."

"Of course, but if you should run into a problem, we are available to help. Just use your cell phone number and we'll be right there. Yes, and do check in with us before you go home. We might have some thing or other for you to take along."

"As you can imagine, Nigel, *nothing* would thrill me more."

Deflecting, Nigel asked, "How old is your nephew?"

"He should be, let's see—about twenty-three by now. I don't know just what he does for a living, but it will be nice to visit with him again."

CHAPTER 12

Visiting His Nephew

Returning to his hotel, Rambar phoned his nephew. "Hello, Patric. This is Uncle Edmund. I'm in London for a few days, just arrived. Aunt Millicent died last week, and I'm here to settle some legal matters. Could we get together for dinner or something? I'd love to see you again. It's been a long time, hasn't it?"

"It's *super* getting to see you again, uncle. Where should we meet and what time? Okay, at my place around 3:00 p.m. You have my address here in Peckham?"

* * *

Before dressing down a bit, he tentatively discarded the sling and tested his arm. With only a little discomfort, he now looked more like an American than an English lord. He checked himself in a mirror, satisfied.

Hailing a taxi, Rambar told the driver, "Take me down to Peckham Road please. I'll show you the building when we get close."

"Oh, bloody hell, not Peckham," the man moaned, beating his forehead against the steering wheel. "Not Peckham. I can neva' get a fare back from there." But knowing he was required to transport a paying passenger to wherever they wanted, he had no alternative. "Aw'right, guv'nr, I'll 'ave you there in a jiffy."

"Don't be upset. I know it's not a great place to pick up a fare, so I'll tip you ten pounds. Will that help?" Edmund asked sincerely.

The driver brightened. "*Super*. Yur a good man, sir."

* * *

Patric had a small flat on the third floor, and Rambar was panting when he reached the top of the stairs. His nephew had heard him and was waiting.

"I'll be moving out of this bloody place soon. I've got a girlfriend who lives over north and we're goin' t' share her place."

"That's lovely, Patric. Tell me all about her."

"She's beautiful and intelligent. She's from the Middle East, been here about two years now."

"Really? Is she a Muslim?"

"Yes, Uncle Edmund...and so am I. Does that disturb you?"

Covering his surprise with an indulgent smile, Rambar said, "Not at all, Patric. I'm far from religious myself. Whatever faith you're comfortable with is the right one for you or anybody else. Good for you. Bravo."

"Are you hungry, Uncle Edmund? I know a *super* Moroccan place just up the way in Camberwell. How does that sound?"

"As you'd say, Patric, it sounds *super*, and I'm famished. Will I have to eat with my fingers or my right hand? Don't want to offend anyone."

* * *

After a short bus ride, they entered the restaurant and was greeted by "Welcome, Mohammad," spoken with a slight accent. "It is so very nice to see you again, and who is this fine gentleman?"

"This is my uncle Edmund from the States, and this is my good friend, Akmed. He owns this place."

Sipping on mint tea and waiting for their food, Patric/Mohammad began. "This must all be surprising to you, uncle, but I really have *found* myself, and I'm *over the top* happy about my life here."

"The only important thing is that you're happy. You have always been my most favorite nephew, even if we're actually just cousins, and I support you in your decisions, always, Pat, er, Mohammad."

"Oh, thank you so much, Uncle Edmund. I could only be happier if you were a Muslim yourself," Patric exclaimed excitedly.

"Well, considering my feelings about religion in general, it would be very unlikely. What type of work are you doing?"

"I'm an assistant to an Imam at a local mosque who's doing some important things to bring the truth of Allah to these infidels. Unfortunately, it's sometimes necessary to do this by unusual methods."

Rambar was now intrigued, not sure just where this was leading. "I see. Yes, sometimes it can be difficult to make people understand different concepts or beliefs."

He was also becoming somewhat apprehensive, thinking that possibly some of these people Patric was involved with could be the same ones hounding him all over London. He decided to try for some specific information while not arousing any suspicion from his nephew.

"Surely these efforts on your part don't involve any anti-government activities, do they? I'd really worry about your safety, Mohammad."

"You shouldn't be concerned, dear uncle. Because I'm doing things to bring the true faith of Allah to these people, he will protect me."

"How do you and your associates go about doing this? Do you hand out pamphlets or something?"

"Our efforts are a lot more sophisticated. Sometimes we are able to apprehend messengers coming into the UK with information valuable to this and other governments-classified stuff."

"That *is* fascinating. How do you even know who they even are?" Edmund pressed gently, showing sincere interest.

"Well, I won't go into specifics, but we have people working in foreign government agencies, I guess they could be called *moles,* who pass information on to us. Didn't you work for the US government yourself, uncle?"

"Oh yes, years and years ago, in the Department of Agriculture. God, what a boring job it was, but I managed to hang in there 'til retirement. Anyway, I got a good pension out of it."

By now, Rambar knew he was on the right track but decided to not press it any further at present. Although sad that his nephew was deeply involved, he would try to get him to divulge more at another time. Quietly angry, he thought to himself, *These are the same damned people who were trying to assault, maybe kill me, for whatever they could find out.*

After dinner, they walked for a short while around Camberwell, looking in a few shops. The weather had become cooler and Rambar hadn't brought his topcoat with him.

"I should call it an evening, Mohammad. I'm a bit chilled, but I'll call you tomorrow afternoon if that's convenient. Perhaps we can have an early dinner somewhere. Do you like seafood? There's a nice fish place near Victoria station."

"That would be *super*, Uncle Edmund. I should be done working by about 4:30 p.m., and I'll wait for your call. Thanks again for dinner, and I'm so glad to see you again."

Back in his hotel room, he called Nigel at MI6. After polite greetings, he dropped the bombshell. "I seem to have bumbled into something very important."

"You sound excited, Edmund. What have you found out?"

"As you recall, I'd mentioned visiting my nephew. This is about him and what he's been up to. We need to meet in person. It's too big a matter to discuss by phone."

"Yes, of course, Edmund. I shall have our taxi come and collect you straight away. Be sure to get into the right one. The number on the door is 1440. Do wear something to identify yourself."

"I'll tie a white pocket hankie around my cane, just below the handle, and will be waiting outside the lobby door of my hotel."

Within minutes, the MI6 taxi arrived and whisked Rambar to Nigel's office.

CHAPTER 13

No Longer His Lordship

Once settled in after a bracing drink of brandy, he began. "As I mentioned on the phone, my nephew is involved in something highly suspicious. He works for a local Imam in a part of London that's effectively under Sharia law. He confided to me that his associates are occasionally able to force couriers to divulge information they are carrying. He didn't tell me how they actually do it, but I suspect it's not given voluntarily."

"Good heavens, man, I think you've stumbled onto something. In fact, these could be the same people who tried to get you at the airport the first time you arrived."

"My own thoughts exactly, Nigel. I'm going to meet my nephew, who now goes by Mohammad, for dinner tomorrow. Let me see what else I can find out from him."

"Quite obviously, we would be more than grateful for whatever you can uncover but do be extremely careful. These people are fanatics, and they play for keeps. In fact, I feel it advisable for you to have some protection immediately available. Unfortunately, both Jack and Helen have been assigned to other cases, but you shall have new people watching you at all times."

With that, Nigel had his assistant come to his office and bring in two new agents. Rambar thought they looked somewhat familiar but couldn't remember from just where. Nigel introduced them as Geoff and Basil.

"You may recall seeing this pair before. Do you know where that was, Edmund?"

"No, I really don't, but I've definitely run across them somewhere. Wait, at the Greek restaurant about a week ago. They were a male couple whom I'd assumed to be gay, is that right?"

"Absolutely correct, old boy. However, they are neither gay nor a couple but were backup agents for Helen and poor Rupert. With something as highly classified as the chip you carried in your denture, we would never trust your protection to only one pair of agents. Of course, we have many undisclosed covert assets as well."

"Well, my most sincere accolades, Nigel. I didn't even remotely suspect they were part of the game. I feel even more assured for my own safety now, and I won't ask if there's a second set of agents watching these two."

At this point, Rambar decided to abandon his lordship persona when he checked out of The Dorchester hotel. It was possible the two Middle Eastern men from the airport had passed along his description. Now he would be just be an older American attending to family business and visiting his British nephew. He was also determined to not limp if he could endure the discomfort of it. He gulped down two more pain pills.

"God, I'd like to be home, petting Hunter and forgetting all about this."

* * *

The next afternoon, a Friday, Rambar met Mohammad at the seafood place near Victoria station for dinner. "Are you comfortable with the fact that I'm now a devout Muslim, Uncle Edmund?"

"Well, of course, I am. It didn't bother me for a minute, Mohammad. You do seem very happy and contented. How is your girlfriend, or perhaps, fiancée?"

"She's very well, and I told her that you are in London. Her name is Ahira, and she would love to meet you."

"Splendid, Mohammad. She sounds absolutely wonderful." Rambar was thinking that she might likely provide even more information than his nephew could. "We must get together very soon because I have to leave for home in two days."

"How about if we meet for lunch tomorrow, Uncle Edmund? Ahira and I could meet you at the Moroccan restaurant in Camberwell. Oh, her aunt will also be along as a chaperone, a Muslim custom, since we are not yet even engaged. The woman does not speak English, but she's a very kind, pleasant person. I think you'll like her."

The next morning, Saturday, Rambar checked out of The Dorchester, ending his masquerade as Lord Chesterton-Rancourt. Now any pursuers, real or imagined, would be following a nonexistent personality. He then taxied over to the less-than-fashionable Earl's Court district and checked into a small boutique hotel near the tube station.

At noon, he was back in Camberwell entering the same Moroccan restaurant his nephew had taken him to previously and being greeted by a genial Akmed. Mohammad and the two ladies, Ahira and her corpulent smiling aunt, arrived a few minutes later.

After ordering and the mint tea was served, a polite small talk began.

"I'm so very pleased to meet you, Ahira, and your charming aunt as well. My nephew has told me many good things about you, especially that you are also a very devout person."

"Yes, Mr. Rambar, he has also told me how very tolerant a man you are. Many people in this world are not as kind or understanding although it is true that Americans are more so than many others. I know that there are many Muslims in the US."

"Indeed, Ahira, and many beautiful mosques."

Continuing on, Rambar appeared congenial and flattering, urging them to call him Uncle Edmund. He asked them to translate for Ahira's aunt, not leaving her out of the conversation.

"I understand that you and Mohammad are doing some very important work in bringing the truths of the Holy Koran to this country."

"We are doing all we can to accomplish this although it is sometimes frustrating. Our efforts are not always successful because others from outside the UK bring in false information about us and spread misinformation as they go." '

Rambar nodded sympathetically.

"As an example," Ahira continued, "only last week, we were very close to apprehending a courier believed to be carrying important documents to that satanic MI6 organization here. We try very diligently to thwart their persecution of us."

"Oh, dear. Tell me what happened. Did the courier evade your people?" Rambar asked innocently.

"Yes, Mr. Rambar, er, Uncle Edmund. It was at Heathrow, that some English aristocrat came back here to the UK. According to one of our contacts, he had information that could have been most useful to us. He even injured one of our faithful and trusted men, breaking his leg. MI6 will use anyone, absolutely anyone, they can."

"That must be frustrating indeed. I wish that I could somehow help your cause, dear ones. I could perhaps contribute some funds to your mosque, or something like that."

"Most kind of you to offer, Uncle Edmund, but we prefer to accept donations only from believers. We would not wish to offend you, a kind man, but you are not a Muslim, as yet. Allah has blessed us with many alms to carry out our work."

"Yes, of course, Ahira, I do understand. It is best to be financed by those who are true believers. While I'm sympathetic to my nephew's causes, it's most unlikely that I would ever become religious at my advanced age."

Ahira smiled and translated the conversation to her aunt who continued eating contentedly. She knew that Ramadan would happen again in a few months, and food or drink could not be taken during daylight hours.

"We have something underway at present that will help us to bring down this ungodly government, if even only in a small way. Allah be praised."

"I know you couldn't give me any details nor would I want you to, Ahira."

"You are a very understanding man, Uncle Edmund. All I can tell you is to *keep your eye on the wheel.* It will become clear to you after the event occurs."

Mohammad shot her a warning glance, shaking his head slightly.

After their meal, Rambar departed, returning to his new hotel room in Earl's Court. Then he called Nigel at MI6. "I need to see you as soon as possible. Have some new information that could be valuable. Oh yes, I'm now staying at the Hotel Calgary in Earl's Court."

CHAPTER 14

The Terrorist's Plan

Getting out of the agency's taxi inside the MI6 garage, Rambar took the elevator up to Nigel's office.

"It's always good to see you, Edmund, and when you bring along some intelligence information, that makes it even better. Would you like a brandy or Drambuie?"

"I'm not sure just when this is going to happen, but let me give you what I have. This is from my meeting just this afternoon with my nephew and his girlfriend, Ahira. She told me to 'keep my eye on the wheel.' What do you think that means, Nigel?"

"Hm, well, it does immediately bring to mind one possibility—the London Eye. You have, no doubt, seen it down by the Thames, as you passed by or when you had that tragic rendezvous along The Embankment. I still regret that Rupert turned out to be a double agent. Quite sad."

Rambar nodded sympathetically.

"However, there may be other meanings to what she said. I'll run it through our WordBot app and see what comes up. It could perhaps refer to the *Five Eyes* intelligence alliance between the UK, the US, Australia, Canada, and New Zealand. Who knows? We'll find out quickly," Nigel continued.

"They apparently thought that the British aristocrat at the airport, me, was bringing in something damaging to their Islamic cause. Were they on the right track with that, Nigel?"

"No, Edmund, nothing of the sort. I believe it is time to provide you with some understanding about that. We are aware that your agency provided you with a top-secret clearance, and we here at MI6 gave you our most secret one as well. Are you familiar with the term REE, Edmund?"

Rambar looked puzzled. "You know how very out of date I am with electronic things, Nigel. What does it mean?"

"It actually refers to Rare Earth Elements, something that most developed countries desperately need. Its uses include the manufacture of cell phones, flat screen televisions, lasers, semiconductors, MRI equipment, even certain light bulbs, to name a few. Then there are the innumerable military uses.

"China has nearly a monopoly on these elements and related critical materials, producing about 80 percent of global output. In addition, they make up over 90 percent of all the yttrium, gallium, and arsenic produced and more than 80 percent of various others.

"So you can see how vital this information can be, Edmund. Quite recently, large deposits of REEs have been discovered in one of the countries that I mentioned before and in Greenland too. Absolutely top-secret stuff. You were carrying this information both on your initial trip over here and then back from Monaco. The French are equally interested.

"Therefore, I can tell you that which you were carrying dealt with a highly critical component of many high-tech applications, which is probably why the Russians were sniffing around trying to find you at the airport in Nice. Somehow, they got word that an English lord was carrying some intelligence of great importance though just exactly what it *was* may have eluded them. We have continual problems with hackers, so we feel couriers are safer."

"Now where do we go from here, Nigel?"

"Let us see what WordBot has come up with, shall we?"

After looking at the printout, he told Rambar, "I believe that I was correct. The most-likely scenario is that they're planning to attack the London Eye. It would be a perfect target for bringing attention to their cause with perhaps hundreds of casualties.

"While London has a huge number of structures and other attractions of greater historical interest, the giant Ferris wheel is a soft target. At any given time, it could contain hundreds of vulnerable tourists. As you may be aware, cyberattacks are effective but don't grab the public's attention as bombings do.

"This is, at least for the moment, a matter for MI5 and the Metropolitan Police. We will immediately notify them both, offering our full assistance and intelligence information, and alert Interpol as well.

"At this point, Edmund, I'm concerned about your safety if you attempt to elicit more information about their activities from either your nephew or Ahira. It's time for you to head home now. You've been of more assistance than MI6 or your agency would have ever considered. Your courier assignment turned out to only be the start, did it not?

"Because of your assistance, we were able to eliminate a mole in our organization and transfer invaluable intelligence between our two countries and to France. We were also able to learn more about ongoing terrorist activities here in London. Thank you so much. All these achievements will be included on our petition to Her Majesty for your honorary knighthood. Well done, Edmund."

"Yes, you're right, Nigel. It's definitely overdue for me to return home. It's been more of an adventure than I would have ever considered doing had I known the full extent. Nevertheless, I'm very pleased that I could still be of some service to both our countries at my age."

"Oh yes, would you take along some information, a microchip, to your people when you return? It seems to be more effective using low-tech methods."

"Aw, Nigel, will this happiness never end? Yes, of course, you know I will. Does it go to the agency [CIA] or to some wonderful place like Zanzibar or Mali as a pleasant side trip? By the way, if you ever happen to be in the United States, try to take a few days off and visit me in Wyoming. You'll always have a place to stay and there are many interesting places to see. We could visit some of the old cavalry forts, see Devil's Tower, walk a bit of the Oregon Trail, and chow down on a buffalo steak."

"In less than three years, I will be retiring and would like to do some foreign traveling. It is entirely possible that I could do just that, so thank you for your kind invitation, Edmund. This assumes, of course, that we both are still alive after these, eh, adventures."

"My plane leaves in the early afternoon, Nigel, and I plan to see my nephew Mohammad, formerly known as Patric, today for a late lunch. If I should happen to learn anything else from that meeting, I'll let you know right away. Otherwise, this is goodbye for a while. It really has been fun now that I think about it, and it got the old juices flowing again. I sort of miss the old days with the agency. Oh, well."

After departing the MI6 building, Rambar realized that he's forgotten to ask Nigel if any shadows would be accompanying him. It did seem routine procedure that they would be provided while he still had classified information with him, but he should have asked.

CHAPTER 15

Encountering His Old Nemesis

At Heathrow Airport, gate 27, Rambar glanced around at the other passengers, an old habit from his days at the CIA. Most of the travelers looked innocuous enough, but his eyes focused on a late middle-aged White male standing across the waiting area. Somewhere he'd seen him before though he couldn't place just where. The man didn't notice or recognize him.

After studying the individual, it dawned on him. This was a Russian operative with whom he had locked horns with many years ago while on a clandestine assignment. The name was coming back to him.

"It's something like Vik...Viktor...Borna...no, Borenko. Yes, that is definitely Viktor Borenko." The Russian had aged. His hair was salt-and-pepper now, and he sported a goatee and moustache. He was thinner than Rambar remembered and probably close to retirement age, maybe sixty-three or sixty-four years old.

Debating whether to openly approach him or depend on the fact that he, himself, had aged sufficiently to go unrecognized, Rambar chose the latter option. He moved over to the crowded bank of chairs, blending into the mass of people waiting for their flight. He took up a conversation with an older woman and her two granddaughters sitting near him. If Borenko happened to glance over his way, he might mistake him for a grandparent on a trip with his family.

The flight was eventually announced, and the elderly and disabled passengers were invited to board first. Rambar stayed close to the grandmother and children, maintaining a casual chat with them. His seat was toward the rear of the 747. In a few minutes, he watched Borenko carefully stow his piece of luggage, an attaché case, under his seat. He sat down in an aisle seat several rows ahead, giving Rambar an unobstructed view during the long flight.

He surmised that the Russian was still on the job and cautiously kept the case with him, touching his heel, instead of in the overhead compartment. After reaching altitude, refreshments were being served by the British Airways flight attendants. He noticed that Borenko ordered a vodka on the rocks and then another.

Many years of training and experience taught him to observe even small details. He noticed that the Russian tied his shoelaces to one side instead of directly in the center of his shoe tops. The man likely suffered from arthritis, causing him some difficulty when tying them.

The flight would take over seven hours, barring a strong headwind, so Rambar could only relax and continue to watch Borenko for other signs of debility. Soon, he observed another symptom. The Russian agent only used his left arm while his right dangled over the seat arm, not being utilized.

Less than two hours into the flight, an announcement came on the intercom.

"This is your pilot speaking. Due to a minor technical problem, we will be landing at a nearby airport, just as a precaution. There is no need for concern whatsoever. We should arrive at the international airport, near Reykjavík, Iceland, in approximately twenty minutes."

Good God, what now? Will I ever get home? Rambar thought mournfully.

He noticed that six rows up, Geoff and Basil were aboard. That was comforting. The plane landed safely, and passengers began departing. As he exited, Geoff touched him and winked.

Inside the terminal, Viktor spotted him and came over. "Are you not the American agent of your government? I'm not remembering your name."

"Yes, but I retired many years ago. Aren't you Viktor…Borenko from the old Soviet Union?"

"You have good memory. Now I think I remember. You are Edvard, or like that, correct?" he asked, mispronouncing Rambar's first name.

"Quite right. Are you still on the job, or are you also retired?"

"For three more years, I work and then would retire and is looking much forward to it. Would you like to have dinner with me and to 'chew the fat,' as they say in US, at Russian Embassy?"

That's all I need, Rambar thought, *to be an unwilling guest at an embassy where the local police have no authority to intervene or rescue me.* "Most kind of you to offer, but since I'm here unexpectedly, I'll call some friends in Reykjavík and visit them."

Borenko frowned slightly.

"So what are you doing in this part of the world, Viktor?"

"Yes, uh...I am here in Iceland to be part of delegation for Russian automobile manufacturer. We sell many of our cars in this country."

"Oh, that's excellent, Viktor. Well, good luck." Rambar knew it was a hastily thought-out lie since this was a nonstop flight to Washington, DC.

An airline representative was awaiting the passengers as they entered the terminal.

"If the aircraft requires time-consuming repairs, our company will cover all costs while you are here in Iceland. Everyone will also receive a complimentary ticket for your next flight on British Airways. We would like to thank you for your patience."

A bus was provided to take passengers to local hotels after it was determined that the plane would require work and have parts flown in. Most opted to stay at the hotel operated by Iceland Airline since it was close to the airline. Rambar decided to try one closer to downtown Reykjavík so he could look around and see the city.

After checking in to the Hotel Ragnarja, he greeted Geoff and Basil, inviting them to dinner with him. He saw Borenko get into a taxi, presumably headed for the Russian Embassy.

I wonder if he knows I'm carrying intelligence information back to the States? Rambar considered.

Having rested and taking pain medication, he joined his two shadows in the hotel dining room. They all ordered reindeer steaks.

"I guess that I'm eating Rudolph or maybe even Bambi," he joked dryly to his companions. "Please call me Edmund, in case I've failed to mention it before."

Over dinner, he briefed them about his adversarial relationship with the Russian agent. "I'm really getting too old to be playing this cat-and-mouse game anymore. Tomorrow is my seventy-ninth birthday, and I would have preferred celebrating at home."

Needing to use the men's room, Rambar excused himself and walked limping down a hallway. He noticed Viktor coming out of an alcove, accompanied by two men in badly fitting suits.

"Edvard, I like for you to meet friends of mine from Embassy. Please to step in here. There are places to sit down while we are talking," he said as he motioned toward the space.

"Hello, Viktor, sorry but I really need to use the toilet right now, then we can talk."

Viktor sighed then glanced toward his companions, signaling that he figured Rambar would return shortly. They sat down back in the alcove, waiting impatiently. Rambar continued walking past the men's room and ducked into a doorway toward the kitchen.

Geoff and Basil realized that it was taking too long for Rambar to return and hurried down the hallway. The Russians had come to the same conclusion and had caught up with him just a few feet short of the kitchen. Viktor pulled out a pistol and pointed it at him.

"We are aware that you carry important documents. Give them to me now."

"Ah, I see that you've acquired a new toy, Viktor, from the Embassy, no doubt. By the way, your English hasn't improved much since I last saw you."

The other two Russians didn't appear to be armed, figuring that an old man would be no problem to subdue.

By now, both Basil and Geoff had reached them, and they *were* armed. Shoving guns into the backs of the two men behind Viktor, they ordered them to lie on the floor. Rambar took advantage of the momentary diversion and weakly managed to knock the weapon out of Viktor's left hand. For good measure, he gave him a somewhat clumsy kick in the shin, knowing that it would disable the arthritic Russian. It did, and he went down.

"Viktor, Viktor, Viktor, is this any way to treat an old friend after all these years? What do you think I have anyway? I told you that I've been retired for years."

Painfully impaired, the Russian was rubbing his shin and cursing in Russian. "Edvard, I will get you for this insult next time we meet, and your Russian is worse than my English, I bet you."

Geoff picked up Viktor's weapon, pocketed it, and told him, "I do say, this is a rather nice weapon. Thank you very much, old boy. Now leave here immediately, you three, and don't ever bother our old friend again."

CHAPTER 16

Rambar Foils Borenko

Upon returning to his room, Rambar immediately noticed that it had been searched. His clothing and papers were strewn everywhere, but unsuccessful, by whoever did it. This time, the microchip was secured in a large ring provided by MI6, which he was wearing. It appeared to have been used for many years, not a new one.

His cell phone rang as he was picking up some of the scattered clothing and documents. "Nigel here, Edmund. Let me update you on what has happened with your nephew and about the plot to destroy the London Eye."

"Yes, I've been wondering how that was going. Did your people manage to foil their efforts?"

"Actually, we've been quite successful with that. We discovered a luggage case filled with C4 explosives and a trigger. It was in the process of being placed within the motor housing of the Wheel itself by two supposed workmen. Using interrogation, we were able to directly connect them with the terrorist cell to which your nephew and his girlfriend, Ahira, belong. A total of eight people have been arrested. I'm sorry, but your nephew was among those charged. They will appear at the Old Bailey Court this coming week. Fortunately, with your great assistance, we were able to take them down before something disastrous occurred. They will not be able to trace any of it back to you because the explosive device was discovered by an employee doing a routine safety inspection."

"Since I'm returning to the States, I couldn't possibly know about any of it. Mohammad/Patric rarely ever writes me anyway, so I'm in the clear, so to speak," Rambar said, relieved. "Oh, another interesting thing, Nigel. An old nemesis of mine, Viktor Borenko, was on the plane with me. It experienced engine trouble, and we had to land in Iceland. He tried, along with two agents from the Russian Embassy, to force me into giving him the information I'm carrying. Your people, Geoff and Basil, overpowered them and sent them running. I did manage to injure Borenko and he's mad as hell at me. I kicked him in his shin, and he fell down, hard."

"Good for you, old boy. Bravo," Nigel cheered. "I've spoken with your CIA people, and they'll have escorts waiting the moment you land in DC."

The next morning, a British Airways plane arrived at the airport to replace the first. Soon, everyone was aboard and underway. Before the flight, Rambar spotted Borenko, who was limping worse than himself. The Russian saw him and scowled menacingly. Edmund nodded and smiled back.

During the turbulent flight, he heard Borenko groan noticeably when the plane hit an air pocket. *Aw, poor guy*, Rambar thought in mock sympathy.

The flight arrived on time and people deplaned quickly. Among them, Borenko hobbled off, looked around for fellow Russian agents, and waited for Rambar to appear. Two dark-suited types connected with Borenko, ready to quickly confront the American. However, about fifty feet inside the exit ramp, three CIA agents, including his friend Larry, met Rambar.

As they entered the gate area, Borenko saw that Rambar had reinforcements with him. His planned effort to grab Edmund was thwarted, and he cursed silently to himself. The two British shadows shook hands with their American counterparts and departed. On leaving, Rambar gave them a grateful smile and handshake.

Upon arriving at CIA headquarters, Rambar turned over the ring containing the intelligence and was debriefed. Larry told him that they had failed to discover the mole within the CIA but had discovered two hackers.

By early evening, exhausted and in considerable leg pain, he retired to his hotel room, still shadowed by two agents. After taking medication and undressing, he collapsed onto the bed, glad it seemed to be over with.

At breakfast the next morning, Rambar met Larry, and they talked spiritedly as old friends. "Edmund, you did a great job, as we all knew you would. Both countries are more than grateful to you. The Russians would have loved getting their paws on that intelligence at any cost.

"Now I can tell you something that you may find damned interesting. We sent out six different couriers, including you. That got our enemies scurrying around, not knowing what it was that they were chasing or even who might be carrying it.

"To be honest, it really was *you* who carried it, which is why our agency went to the great effort of hiding it in your denture. The other five couriers carried only some dummy information of no value and were instructed to give it up if they were in danger. Oddly enough, none of them were even approached. I believe it was because of the *mole* in our agency that they focused on you so quickly. Anyway, all's well that ends well because of your cleverness and that you were under constant surveillance.

"Our Russian friends know that whatever you were carrying is now in safe hands, so they won't be bothering you on your trip home. But you did really piss off Borenko when you kicked the crap out of his leg, so he might try getting even. We have a couple of tricks planned to throw him off your trail since he doesn't know where you live."

"My car is here at the Denver airport, and I was just going to drive back home, Larry. What little tricks do you have in mind?"

"First, we'll have one of our people drive your car back to Wyoming, using a circuitous route, just in case. Then we'll take you home in an agency vehicle using deception by disguising you as someone else. Until we know for sure who's the mole in our organization, we won't tell anyone except for our low-level transportation people. None of them have access to operational information or missions."

CHAPTER 17

Offered Training Job

Larry decided to drive Edmund back to Wyoming so they'd have a chance to talk and evaluate how the mission went, a debriefing of sorts. Rambar was disguised in a cowboy hat, a bandanna around his neck, and Western jacket and boots. With a fake gray moustache, he looked like an elderly ranch owner or foreman.

"With all your experience and ability to improvise in dangerous situations, the agency could benefit greatly if you were an instructor for our rookie agents. I'm not thinking of a full-time position in Langley, Virginia, or anything, just occasional freelance work if and when needed.

"You have a lot to offer, something that few of our trainers have, with your many years of field experience. Despite the fact that you're older than dirt, you've just completed a difficult assignment that we didn't dare entrust to anyone else. More than that, your low-tech approach and creativity to these clandestine operations is coming back into vogue. It's so absurd and out-of-date that it's probably the safest manner of conveying highly classified intelligence."

"Hm," Rambar replied. "There's so many complicated techniques and methods being used now like drones, cyber warfare, underground bases, hypersonic gliders, and dozens of other new things. I think I'm too out-of-date to be of much use now, don't you?"

"No, not really, Edmund. We'd like you to inspire young operatives to think creatively, to improvise, and to show them how to create disguises on short notice."

"Well, I'll think about it, Larry. I'll think about it."

They pulled into the driveway of Rambar's house, and Larry helped him carry in his luggage, which included the custom-made suits and other clothing from London.

"I'll check back with you in a week or two, okay, Edmund? But take however long you want to decide. We'd really like to have you back on the team."

"Sure, Larry, give me a call whenever. It's always great talking with an old friend. I will think about the offer. Now I want to get my dog and see Loretta, so *hasta la* bye-bye."

As Larry waved to him and departed, Rambar started walking over to Loretta's place, carrying the perfume he'd bought for her in Monaco. Strangely, his bad knee wasn't bothering him at all. His relief at being home again and seeing Hunter filled his thoughts completely.

As he approached, Hunter's keen hearing started him barking. Loretta opened her front door as his dog bounded out to greet him with overwhelming excitement. The large animal leaped up, putting his front paws on Rambar's chest, nearly knocking him backward, and frantically licking his face with slobbery kisses.

Fearing he might drop the small gift for Loretta, he smiled broadly and handed it to her. With Hunter between them, she leaned in and gave Rambar a friendly peck on the cheek, which he happily returned. They hugged warmly.

"I'm so relieved that you're back home, Edmund. I don't know just why, but I've been so worried about you ever since you let me know about going on to London from Toronto. Was it woman's intuition, a premonition, or what?"

"I have a lot to tell you about, Loretta, but mostly that I thought of you so often and missed you more than I realized. Also thought that I'd be completely exhausted by now, but I feel somehow exhilarated."

"Well, come on in, and I'll put on some coffee and we can talk."

By now, Hunter had calmed down and settled in next to Rambar in the living room, still looking at him with adoring eyes.

As Loretta brought in coffee and some cookies she'd made, she said, "Please tell me everything, Edmund. Were you in some kind of danger over there?"

"Well, first, you remember me telling you that I worked for the government some years ago. It was the Central Intelligence Agency, the CIA. Recently they offered me an opportunity to work a onetime assignment for them. It involved paying me quite well for doing it. In fact, it was an offer that I couldn't refuse, considering how much money I'd give to my son and daughter-in-law to buy their house.

"While I can't go into every detail, it involved me taking something to the UK with a stop in Toronto, en route. As you know, I made it to London, did my thing, and then had time to see my nephew Patric. Oh, did you get the food basket from Harrods?"

"Yes, and it was wonderful, Edmund. I still have some of the things left. It was a huge parcel. UPS delivered it in perfect condition too. Then what happened?"

"Well, they were so pleased in London that I'd got the information over to them safely, MI6, similar to our CIA, decided to reward me with a few days in the south of France, in Monaco, to be exact. So with everything paid for, I flew down to Nice."

"Just where is Nice at, Edmund? I've never been very good with geography."

"It's on the Mediterranean, a few miles west of Monaco. Anyway, there was one condition for me to get this reward. I was to carry something with me to deliver once I got there, which I did. So the next three days were spent sightseeing, and that's where your perfume is from. Princess Grace encouraged local industry including the company that produces it. Hope you like the scent all right."

"It will be wonderful, just knowing that you were thinking of me and because you're safely home again."

"I was going to fly back to London," Rambar continued, "but had a strange feeling about it, so I took the high-speed train up to Paris instead. That flight crashed just north of Nice, killing everyone. There was a bomb on board."

At this, Loretta got up, hugged Edmund, and gave him another longer kiss.

"Please don't do these dangerous things. I love you so much." Then trying to lighten the mood and avoid crying, she joked weakly, "Well, I would still have had Hunter, of course, and I do like him even more than you, but still…"

* * *

Back home at his place, Edmund poured himself a Drambuie on the rocks and looked at all the custom clothes he'd been given.

"Not a bad haul, especially with the $400,000 I got. Maybe I'll do it again, or not."

Hunter woofed *his* agreement.

CHAPTER 18

An Experienced Instructor

About two weeks later, Larry called. "Edmund, you old rascal, have you been thinking about our agency's offer to teach?"

"Well, yeah, I have been mulling it over, Larry. The first thing is this, why should I consider doing it at all? I don't need the money and, obviously, I'd need to drive to somewhere else to do any teaching. Or could I do it remotely, however that all works?"

"The agency is more than willing to make it as convenient for you as possible, including some remote instruction. However, you would need to do a certain part in person like for field exercises, the practical applications. Oh, before I forget, we found our mole or, at least one of 'em, in case there could be more. We don't think so, though."

"That's encouraging," Edmund replied with some relief. "So on the positive side, I do feel some degree of obligation to be useful and do whatever I still can to help out. After all, by doing my bit recently, I realized that I still *have it together* enough to play the game, and I kind of missed it. Yeah, you're right, Larry, this is something that you never really retire from. Here's what I'd be willing to do.

"Every two weeks, I could teach for two days in person, consecutively, either in Cheyenne or Casper at one of the field offices. Then if you can set it up, I'd do two more days remotely from my house, right after my two days done live. Four days total every two weeks is about all I could handle. The salary would be at the same grade level as when I retired. Carrying a concealed weapon might be useful too. What do you think?"

"I think our agency would be damned glad to get you at all. Your terms are no problem, and our physical trainers would do all the rough stuff. You'd just do the *Sneaky Pete* part. If you feel better carrying, that's no problem. You are a CIA agent when you're working."

* * *

The next week, Rambar, dressed in one of his new suits from London, was introduced to a class of new operatives by Larry. They have just graduated from basic instruction, and this series of sessions would be called *Improvisational Techniques.*

"This is one of our most esteemed and highly capable operatives, Edmund Rambar. He has just completed an assignment of great importance to our country. Although he's technically retired, we still call on him for situations requiring his unique capabilities." Thus, Larry introduced him to a class of newly minted agents.

There were five males and one was female, all soon to be fully trained. Most were in their early to midtwenties, and they looked somewhat doubtful at this old man standing in front of them. To them, he appeared to have been retired for at least a good thirty years or longer.

"I think you will all understand what a true master of disguise he is when I tell you that he's actually thirty-seven years of age," Larry stated with a pseudo-serious look on his face. The student agents gasped.

"Thank you, Larry. I think that got everyone's attention. Seriously though, I'm not in a disguise at the moment, this is the real me. Again, my name is Edmund Rambar. Let's get something out of the way right now. As you can see, I'm older than most countries and only slightly younger than God. However, having just completed an assignment that required resourcefulness and mental acuity, I feel that I'm still *with it* and trust that you will agree with me by the end of these sessions.

"The first thing to tell you is this: knowledge is not wisdom but combined with experience. It is vital to any task being undertaken. No one can successfully complete an assignment without basic know-how. You folks have the tools, and now you will begin to gain the experience.

"It is difficult to pick up any skills by only listening. Nevertheless, some can be absorbed by hearing the experience others have gained from situations they've been in. This is why I'm here today and for several additional sessions, both in person and virtually. Along with those, I'll be accompanying you individually on field exercises after the lecture portion is completed.

"Covert operations often involve much subtlety. These can be as simple as signals between operatives and informants to indicate actions to be taken. They can also inform their fellow agents to break contact, depart an area, and many other things. I know you learned this in your basic training at Langley.

"Building on that, another aspect of covert ops is disguises, which are quick to effect in hostile situations. This, I believe, was not covered. Am I correct?" Several heads nodded in agreement. "The main purpose of disguising yourself is to throw off the enemy who may be shadowing you. This technique is not as difficult or intricate as it might seem.

"If you can change two or three characteristics about your appearance while momentarily out of sight of your pursuer, this can be the disconnect moment. You can successfully cause doubt that they are following the right person by three things: size, shape, and color. First, you can change your size to appear thinner by shedding clothing or heavier by adding something. A pillow tucked inside your shirt, pants, or dress can make you look portly or pregnant. This latter is only recommended for female agents, of course. Your creativity will develop all sorts of ways to do this.

"Second, changing shape and how to do it. If you are wearing a topcoat, a hat, gloves, etc., you can discard them the moment that you are not being observed. Now you have perhaps only a tropical shirt, a sport coat, a pair of slacks, or a blouse and skirt on, if wearing a hat, take it off. Then put on sunglasses, a scarf, a bandanna, or whatever you might have handy.

"A bit later, I'll explain the items I normally carry in my disguise kit, and it's very minimal, flat, and easy to tote around. Back to the third element, color. You can wear something bland and nondescript, like gray, beige, tan, or sometimes even black. Anything which can be shed to reveal a brightly colored outfit will often be adequate to confuse the person/s trailing you. Coupled with the accoutrements I mentioned, sunglasses, even an antibacterial mask or a pipe, you can usually shake them off. Having an older-type camera around your neck gives you a tourist appearance.

"Obviously, there is some overlap in the things I've just discussed. What should your disguise kit contain? Tell me a few of the things you might put into it."

Several suggestions were advanced. Fake facial hair, sunglasses, darker-skin lotion, an arm band, scarf, a wig, and several others were mentioned.

"Very good, everyone. Also consider having an inflatable pillow-type item you can quickly blow up, a foldable cane, and a travel sticker to put on your luggage, representing the country or an organization your disguise appears to be from. For example, when I was disguised as someone from India, a sticker on my suitcase which said *Visit India* added credibility.

"Also, don't forget about your shoes. Always wear something that won't attract undue attention. Plain black or brown works well. Avoid saddle shoes, open-toed styles, or anything that glitters. If you effect a disguise that requires footwear specific to that area, then carry cloth slipovers to change the shape of the shoes.

"Together, all these things might weigh a pound or two, in a container separate from other things in your luggage, and always a carry-on, never checked. Keep them handy because you never know when you might need to change your appearance.

"Please understand that the few items you might carry in your kit will not allow you to create an endless number of disguise characters. Decide on three or four to create quickly and practice using them a few times. On my most recent assignment, I was an Indian, an Orthodox Jew, a Western rancher, and an English aristocrat.

"Even without using anything from your kit, you can modify your appearance in several ways. Wearing a plain color suit or sport coat, turn up the collar or carry it over your arm. A casual jacket, if reversable, can be turned inside out, exposing completely different colors.

"Start putting together your own kit tonight, and we can review what each of you have in a day or two. You can learn from your fellow operatives here. We may use these in our practical portion when my lectures have been completed. The next session will deal with *deception.*"

* * *

At the end of the afternoon lecture, four or five of the young aspiring operatives were standing around, smoking or having a soft drink and hashing over what they had been told.

"Aw, I don't know. He's been out of this a long time and an old fart. It's probably just a waste of our time. I want to get out and really do some actual spy work, not sit around listening to some old geezer," one of the young men groused.

At this point, Larry came around a corner of the building. He'd been taking in their conversation, evaluating their reactions. He was not happy with that remark, and his face was visibly flushed as he approached the speaker.

"Listen, junior, I've worked with Mr. Rambar longer than you've been alive, and he's brilliant. There is probably no one in the agency who knows more about covert ops than he does, and he's forgotten more about it than you'll learn in your next thirty years.

"Before you were even hatched, he was doing damned important work out of the Caravelle Hotel in Saigon. You may not know anything about that unless it was mentioned when you were at Langley learning the basics. It was the operations center for ours and several other agencies in Vietnam, and Mr. Rambar was its most important operative. So if you think you can't learn anything from his decades of experience, you can pack up your crap and head home right now, kid."

"Look, I'm sorry…Larry. I really didn't mean anything by it. I was just making a comment."

"In the first place, junior, my name is not Larry to you. It's *sir* until you complete the training by Mr. Rambar, which is how you will address him. Do you understand?"

"I'm very sorry…sir. I'll keep my big mouth shut."

CHAPTER 19

Training Rookies

"Continuing on, before we get into discussing *deception*," Rambar began with the next day's class, "it is critical that you have prepared a *cover story* to support your assumed persona. For example, if you are in disguise as a Belgian diplomat, you should be able to speak both French and Flemish to some degree.

"It is entirely possible that someone might challenge you in a seemingly casual conversation. If you don't happen to have that ability, your *cover* will unwind quickly, and you may be unable to recover any credibility. In other words, your *cover* will be blown, and you will need to beat a hasty retreat.

"Assuming that you are conversant in the appropriate lingo, you had best know the location and address of the embassy, consulate, or whatever place you claim to represent. If your questioner asks if you know a certain so-and-so named whatever, most likely it will be a trap. You could explain that you just arrived at that post only a week ago and don't know that person.

"There are so many ways that you can be tripped up, so know the culture you pretend to be from, including a few customs, important events, people from that country, and so forth. Also, try to go on the offensive and begin asking them questions or whatever to shift the spotlight off yourself."

* * *

On his third day of classroom lectures, still in person though not planned that way, Rambar greeted his neophyte operatives. "Good morning, group. Let me see if I have your names correctly. You are Jared, temporarily referred to as *Junior* by Larry, as he mentioned to me. However, that was only a onetime gaff, and to me, as well as the other class members, you are Jared. Agreed?"

"Yes, sir, Mr. Rambar, and I really hope you will disregard any thoughtless comments I made outside of class."

"Next, Chanthini, am I right? You have the most beautiful name. Are you from India or your parents?"

Actually, she told him that she was a first generation American and both parents are naturalized citizens.

"You must be Malcolm, and with a British-sounding name, you probably have one persona that is quite natural, don't you?"

"Yes, sir, Mr. Rambar, I have a lot of relatives living in the UK, but I was born in Seattle. I've spent some time in England, most of it when I was a teenager."

Then Rambar identified David, a young man from Louisiana; George, an Asian; and Derek, a New Yorker.

"If you happen to be approached by an American or Canadian, and you don't want to speak with them for some reason, you can always lapse in some semblance of another language. Most North Americans tend to be monolingual except for many Latinos.

"On one occasion, I was in the Gare du Nord railway station in Paris when I was approached by a rather large, loud, and obnoxious American woman wearing shorts, a Hawaiian blouse, and three cameras around her neck. Immediately, giving no greeting whatsoever, she began with 'Hey, do ya know where th' subway is from here?'

"Feeling somewhat irritated by her manner, I gave her a blank look and said, '*Je regret, madame, mais je n'parle pas Anglais.*' She gave me an exasperated frown and told her daughter, 'This son of a bitch can't even speak English!' It was difficult to suppress a laugh as they hurried away. Now on to *deception*, using your imagination, the possibilities are endless. Here are a couple of examples.

"If you duck out of the sight of someone following you, even for a minute, quickly take off your hat, put on sunglasses, take off your jacket, etc. Then find someone to appear that you are walking with. Some years back, I felt that someone was trailing me.

"Fortunately, I spotted an elderly woman who was having difficulty carrying her luggage. So I quickly asked her if I could be of assistance. She agreed, and we came around a corner looking like perhaps grandmother and grandson. Whoever was following me was thrown off completely.

"If you know beforehand that you might be trailed, you could enlist the help of another agent or even a dog. Once your pursuer spots you, immediately get out of his or her sight, ditch the companion or give them the dog, and you will be alone at next sight. Again, the ways are limitless. Just use your *little gray cells*, to quote Hercule Poirot, of the Agatha Christie novels.

"I knew a large African American guy years ago who used to run around Mexico City, cruising hotel lobbies. Wearing a purple dashiki, he would introduce himself as the ambassador from Mozambique and score free drinks or a lunch from unsuspecting tourists or business people. Rarely was he ever challenged because hardly anyone knew much about that country, or even Africa, for that matter. Again, he did know something about the culture there. Now let's look at the disguise kits you've put together. Ladies first. How about you, Chanthini?"

Having placed several items into average-sized plastic box, she began laying things out. There was a blond wig, sunglasses, a large crushable sun hat, a brightly colored scarf, shoe covers, a jar of skin-lightening makeup, a small inflatable pillow, travel stickers, a bright luggage strap, large rubber bands, a clanking charm bracelet, a large but lightweight camera, a small vial of pepper, and a book.

Noting each item that she had laid out, Rambar looked pleased. "Tell us what the rubber bands and the pepper are for please, Chanthini."

"The rubber bands can be used to hold sleeves or trouser legs up higher, creating a different shape of clothing. Or if needed, they could be snapped toward some object as a diversion. The pepper could be blown toward someone to make them sneeze while you escape."

"Excellent, Chanthini. You've definitely thought this out very well. As time goes on, we think of other useful items to include. These kits evolve as our situations change. One could also have the book hollowed out to contain other things too, perhaps a second passport or whatever."

Then the other student agents opened the disguise kits they'd assembled for Rambar's appraisal. Jared included similar items but geared for a male, as did the other men.

At this time, Larry entered the room with another middle-aged man who looked distinguished. He was carrying a small portfolio. "Let me interrupt your group for a moment," Larry said by way of introduction. "This is Consul General Michael Edward Adkinson from the British consulate in Denver. He is here to make a presentation."

"Thank you very much. Now let me ask Mr. Rambar to step over by me please." Edmund walked over next to him, slightly puzzled. "Dear Mr. Rambar, on behalf of Her Majesty, Queen Elizabeth II, I am genuinely honored to bestow upon you an honorary knighthood of the British Empire for your recent and most important work in providing a great measure of vital intelligence information to her realm. The British people offer their sincere congratulations to you."

With that said, he handed Rambar a leather-bound certificate imprinted with the Royal Seal and the queen's signature. It was impressively hand-illuminated in the ancient manner.

Being that Rambar is American and employed by a Federal agency, a formal knighthood could not be offered, but along with the certificate, there was a check drawn on the Bank of England, as had been promised by Nigel at MI6.

Perhaps not previously having grasped the huge importance of what Mr. Rambar had accomplished for both the American and British governments, the students stood there wide-eyed with open mouths and a singular thought. He was a genuine hero.

"Unfortunately, as an employee of the Federal government, I'm not allowed to accept any gifts whatsoever. However, with permission of your government," Rambar said politely, turning toward the consul general, "I would like to present this check to a wonderful

86

British charity. They rescue work horses from Middle Eastern countries and take them to the UK. There they can live out their final days peacefully grazing in country fields. Otherwise, they would be worked until the day they drop from exhaustion."

"What a kind and beautiful gesture, Mr. Rambar. On behalf of that charity and the British government, we thank you most sincerely."

CHAPTER 20

Field Exercises

For the next few weeks, Rambar drove down to Cheyenne two days every other week and then another two days virtually. It was now time to begin the field training scenarios. Unfortunately, for Rambar, these couldn't be done in Cheyenne, so he was flown down to Denver on a commercial plane. He scheduled them for two days each week, taking out one student operative at a time.

An abandoned hotel building had been leased by the agency for training purposes. Signs were posted *entry forbidden* in case homeless people might try to get inside. Electronic surveillance was set up for the same purpose and so the other student agents could observe the exercise.

Jared was the first man selected to show off his skills. His assignment was to enter the building undetected, determine where a simulated terrorist cell was meeting, hypothetically in some foreign country, then attempt to install a microphone and TV monitor close by and leave undetected.

"Okay, Jared, how would you go about this from start to finish?"

"First, I'd coordinate with the local police so they wouldn't check into what was happening and possibly even blow our surveillance activities. Then I'd enter the building from a side or rear entrance, preferably unobserved by tenants of nearby buildings or pedestrians in the area.

"After determining which floor the terrorists might be on, I'd find a room next to where they're at and, if unlocked, enter it. If the door was secured, I'd quickly pick the lock and enter. Listening at an air duct, I'd attempt to determine how many people were next door. Ideally, I could hear voices and activity, but failing that, I could look out the window and try to see if there was also one for the next room. Then I would try to hear any voices or movement.

"With luck, their window might be slightly open, and I could put a microphone or TV monitor on the outside windowsill. Since these devices are very small, they could easily be placed unnoticed. If that window is too far away to reach, then I'd try for an electrical wall outlet. The wiring will usually place these back-to-back, facing both rooms. Removing the plate cover, I'd install a microphone if I could hear voices from the other room.

"I should also mention that I'd be dressed like a street person in case they found me. Then I'd act disoriented, drunk, or sick, giving indications of getting ready to vomit. It could be useful to carry a bottle of booze and spill some on my clothes or drink a swig before they get to me.

"Although it would be riskier, I could stumble into their room, acting intoxicated, to see who and how many there were. Mumbling drunkenly, I'd say, 'Who the hell are you...p-people, and w-where am I?'

"They'd likely be caught off guard momentarily, and I'd stumble back out, maybe dropping my liquor bottle, saying, 'Oh...I'm-m sorry. W-w-wrong room. Chanthini's idea of having some pepper handy is a good one, or I might carry some pepper spray to use if they try to grab me. Then I'd get the hell out of there, fast."

"Okay, Jared, very good. Now have you missed anything? For example, when walking up the stairs in an old building, they tend to creak. You can avoid this by walking carefully on the sides, staying away from the middle. This is also true when walking along a hallway. Stay close to the walls and avoid the center of thresholds in doorways.

"When you're acting drunk and just barge in isn't so important, but normally, you'd stand to the side of a doorway instead of in front to avoid being shot at. I'm sure this was covered at Langley, but as I learned in Latin class, *repetatcio est mater de studiorium.*

"Overall, your exercise was successful, having done all you could secretly and then having a simple cover story in case you were discovered. Good job, Jared."

* * *

Over the following weeks, Rambar guided his charges through different field scenarios then evaluated their performance. In one, Derek did a quick appearance shift, using a Greek fisherman's cap he'd included in his disguise kit. Being of dark complexion, it was especially convincing when he roughed up his light-colored shirt and smeared some dirt on it and his jeans. Then he splashed water under his arms to give the appearance of a sweating manual laborer. He also carried around some building materials for a while. The scenario consisted mainly of just blending in with a large group of working men on a building project.

This time, Rambar decided to take Hunter, his dog, and visit some friends in Denver, so he drove the 140 miles to the city. At about 1:00 p.m., after a field exercise with Chanthini, he decided to take her for lunch in nearby Larimer Square. It was a warm late winter day, and accompanied by Hunter, they dined outside in an upscale restaurant.

A few tables away but inside the place, a man was looking out the large window. He couldn't believe his luck. There was Rambar sitting with an Indian-appearing young woman having lunch. The bright sun prevented anyone from looking back into the restaurant.

"That son of a bitch. I'll get him this time," he mumbled half to himself and to the other two men with him. He quickly told them about his previous encounters with the former (as he believed) CIA agent. It was Viktor Borenko. He was in Denver as part of a delegation to set up a Russian consulate in the city. A sufficient number of ex-patriots and businessmen now lived there to warrant opening a new diplomatic post. The fact that he had run across his old nemesis, Rambar, was purely accidental.

When Rambar and Chanthini left the restaurant, Borenko and his associates followed at a distance. Inside the nearby parking ramp, the pair with dog in tow, reached their car.

Suddenly Borenko approached them, shouting angrily, "Edvard, you bastard, I get you now!"

Having just opened the door fully to let Hunter into the back seat, he heard and then saw the Russian running toward him, cursing. As he stopped just outside the door and reached toward Rambar, he stumbled backward as the door hit him flatly. Hunter leaped out of the car, on the attack. On the passenger's side, Chanthini looked momentarily confused as to what was happening.

"This is no drill, Chanthini. This man is trying to kill me!" Rambar yelled at her.

Immediately she understood and saw one of the other Russians coming at her. She swung her purse at his face, then followed up by driving her knee forcefully into his groin. He crumpled toward the concrete floor. Realizing this would only stop him briefly, she doubled up her fist, reached down, and slammed it into his right temple. He remained down, dazed.

Then Chanthini calmly dialed 911 on her cell phone and told the police dispatcher what was happening and their location.

By now, the third Russian had reached Rambar and struck him a glancing blow. This was a bad mistake. Hunter leaped, knocking him down and fiercely biting him while savagely scratching at his face with his claws. Unfazed by the slight contact, Rambar grabbed his cane and went after his assailant, striking his solar plexus firmly. He dropped down in sharp pain and drooled onto the pavement.

Borenko had partially recovered and was standing unsteadily on his feet. Rambar whacked him on the neck with his cane, and the Russian slumped on the car's front fender, grabbing at his throat.

Unknown by Rambar, Chanthini had a small .22-caliber pistol in her purse, and by now, she had it out, pointing it at the other still dazed Russian assailant.

"If you move, Viktor, my partner will…blow your brains out, so stay where you are…or die. I've told you before, this…is not a… nice way to act," Rambar cautioned him while trying to catch his own breath. "Oh, Chanthini, you are such a...naughty girl carrying...a hidden weapon and not telling me, but...*thank you* most...sincerely," he chided her while he smiled gratefully, still gasping for air.

With siren on, a Denver police cruiser screeched to a stop and two officers jumped out.

"All right, what's going on here?" the sergeant asked Rambar.

"These men attacked us. I...am...a CIA operative and so is...this young woman," he replied, still trying to breathe fully. "Here is...my ID. These are Russians, and...they're trying to kill me. As you can see, we were...just barely able to fight them off."

Chanthini also showed the officers her ID, and they acknowledged them as friendlies.

Borenko had regained some composure and mumbled, "We are Russian citizens, and we are claiming diplomatic immunity. You cannot arrest us."

"Sure, sure, now get in the patrol car," the sergeant said as he and his partner handcuffed all three.

It would take several hours at the Denver police station for the Russians to be released under the diplomatic immunity provision. Even then, they had some minor injuries that needed medical attention. By then, Rambar and Hunter would be safely back across the Wyoming border.

CHAPTER 21

Back Home Briefly

After visiting some friends in Lakewood, a major suburb just west of Denver, Rambar and Hunter headed home. They agreed that his master should drive since Hunter only had a dog license, not a driver's license. Going north on freeway I-25, they purposely stopped at a few rest areas to be sure they weren't followed.

Rambar wasn't certain if the Russians had managed to get his Wyoming plate number during the scuffle although he doubted they had. Nor was it likely they would have known where he had gone since they were hauled off by the police and then went to an emergency room. So he'd wait a few minutes each time to see if a suspicious looking car pulled into the parking area. None did. Then both Hunter and Rambar needed to stop. His dog using the pet-walking section, and he went into the men's room.

Refreshed, they continued north, but to be doubly sure, Rambar turned west at the Fort Collins off-ramp and waited to see if another vehicle did the same. Secure that they were not followed, they arrived back at home by early evening.

Both were tired although Rambar was definitely more so. He tumbled down on his bed after feeding Hunter. They would go over and see Loretta in the morning.

She always faithfully collected his mail and had it waiting in a neat pile when he returned. Loretta greeted him with a smile and a treat for Hunter. She hugged Edmund warmly and then poured coffee for him.

"I'm always a bit worried when you drive down to Denver. It must get tiring for you, doesn't it?"

"It's odd, but I really feel energized by still being useful to the agency and helping young agents gain experience. Of course, the drive does get tiresome, but normally, they fly me down there from Cheyenne. It'll all be done with in a couple more weeks or so. Once I get this group through my class, it'll be over as far as instructing. With this kind of business, though, you're never really retired, so who knows what will come up in the future."

"Eventually you'll have to give it up, won't you, Edmund? After all, you are eighty, and from what you've said, or *not* said, it can be dangerous work."

"Oh yeah, there comes an end to everything, and my old bones constantly let me know that I'm done with the physical stuff. Now it's only instructing, not much else," he half lied, not wanting to worry her. "Hunter enjoyed his outing, but I probably won't take him again while I'm doing the teaching. As I mentioned, it's only a few more weeks. Besides, I'm only a young seventy-nine, not eighty.

"I still have three of the young agents to do field exercises with yet. I take them out in simulated scenarios to see what they can do in handling situations which require quick thinking and ability to improvise. These are really a lot of fun for me as well as them."

When he returned home, the phone rang. It was Larry in Denver.

"I heard you had a big scuffle with the Russians again and that you and Chanthini, oh, and Hunter, really kicked the tar out of 'em. You've got to get a less arduous hobby, you know. A man your age shouldn't be doing that. Anyway, the reason I called, other than to congratulate you, is to tell you about a really good scenario for your next field exercise. Let's see, you're going to have Malcolm with you on the next one, aren't you, on Monday?"

"Right you are, Larry, and I'll bet you guys down there have come up with a real doozy, haven't you?"

"Naw, this one's straight out of Langley, and it's kind of import- ant. I'll fill you in on the details when you get here, not on the phone, even though you're still using the secure crypto one. Are you going to bring Hunter down this time or coming alone?"

"I'm flying this time, so if you'll have someone pick me up at the airport as usual, I'd appreciate it. Hunter won't be coming with me this time. My neighbor Loretta will babysit him again. They love each other."

* * *

As Rambar was pouring his favorite drink, a Drambuie on the rocks, the phone rang again. This time it was his son, Bob, calling from Phoenix. "Hi, Dad, haven't talked with you for a while. How's everything going up there? Good! I'm going to be in Denver in a few weeks, and I'd like to come up and see you, okay?"

"You know it's always wonderful to see you, son. When do you think you'll be in Denver? How is Sandra? By the way, I'm doing some teaching for my old outfit and some is done in Denver. If it works out timewise, we could get together there instead of you having to drive all the way up here."

"I don't have the exact date yet, Dad, but most likely in early April. Would that work out okay for you? Hey, aren't you supposed to be retired, why the teaching?"

"That could definitely work out. In fact, I'll *make* it work unless you really want to come here and see how lax my housekeeping is. Of course, if you did get up here, then you could meet my lady friend Loretta. The agency made me a good offer to do a series of classroom and some virtual teaching. As you well know, one can never have enough money. Besides it's only temporary, just for a few weeks, and they usually fly me down there, so I don't need to drive."

CHAPTER 22

The Rock Band

In Larry's office, as he and Rambar slurped down some coffee accompanied by a fresh prune Danish, he explained the planned field exercise. "There is a new rock band from England called *The Trafalgar Palanquin*, and they're making their first USA performance here in Denver. It will be the British Invasion II.

"Their lead singer is named Tommy Venom, talk about a weird name, and he's a distant relative of Nigel's at MI6. Anyway, he's going to be carrying a CD for us, a really important one. We want you to go over to the Rocky Mountain Concert Center with Malcolm to contact him and get that CD. There'll be a British undercover guy accompanying him to be sure it gets here all right, but he'll stay anonymous.

"You can play it any way you want, but Malcolm could be your grandson and a big fan of Tommy and his band. Here are two backstage passes to get you both in tonight before the show starts. Give Malcolm a quick briefing and make sure he plays it up *big* about being a fan. Tommy will recognize you because you'll be the only *elder geezer* there. He'll have the CD ready to give to Malcolm as he often does for fans."

* * *

Rambar arrived at 6:45 p.m. with Malcolm in tow, and they showed their passes to the guard at the stage entrance. He looked at them curiously, wondering why such an old man would show up to see a rock group.

Rambar picked up on it and explained, "My grandson here is a great fan of the *Trafalgars*, and Tommy invited him over here tonight."

The guard nodded and opened the stage door for them.

Inside, they headed for the stage where the band was practicing. Tommy spotted them and walked over to greet them. "Hallo. You mus' be Malcolm. C'mon over and meet me, mates, an' you too, gramps," he said in his Cockney accent.

"Would you mind if I took a few pictures of you and your band? You're all such nice guys," Rambar asked politely.

"No, gramps, y'go ahead. We loves 'aving our pictures taken," Tommy said.

After meeting a few of the band members, Tommy got out a CD for Malcolm. About to hand it over to him, another member of his group said, "Eh, you don't want to be givin' this nice young chap one of our old ones now, do ya?" he said as he grabbed the CD from Tommy.

Reacting quickly, Malcolm realized that was *the very CD* he needed to get from Tommy! "Oh no, I'd like to have that one too and your newest one, if it's okay," he said as he managed to retrieve the first one from the friendly but grabby band member.

Rambar sighed, quietly relieved. Tommy shook hands with Malcolm and his "grandfather."

"I'd lov' t' chat you blokes up some more, but I've got some last-minute practicing t' do. Sorry."

"God, that was close," Rambar said quietly as they left. "Quick thinking, Malcolm. You did really good, and I got some pictures for our classmates to study."

The band was going full blast as they got to the stage door.

"It's fortunate that we're leaving. I couldn't take too much of that horrible screeching." Rambar commented, pretending to cover his ears.

"Sure, Mr. Rambar. Sure," Malcolm replied, rolling his eyes.

After briefly conferring with Rambar back at the CIA field office, Larry shook hands with both men. Malcolm presented the CDs to Larry, explaining that one was just rock music, but the other was the important secret stuff.

"Edmund, er, Mr. Rambar tells me you did an excellent job on this, Malcolm. The agency needs sharp young people who can think on their feet. Good for you," Larry praised him sincerely.

"Tomorrow morning, I'll take Jorgé out and see how he does. Everyone's started calling him George. He's a good student, and he speaks fluent Spanish too," Edmund told Larry. "Do you have any more field scenarios dreamed up, or shall I go with what I have in mind?"

"Nope, you're the professor, Edmund. Whatever you've cooked up will be just fine with us at the agency," Larry assured him.

CHAPTER 23

The Rookie Rescue

The next morning, Tuesday, Jorgé was ready for his first field exercise accompanied by Rambar. They headed over to the west side of the city to the Far East Center, a shopping area for the predominantly Asian people in the area. There were also considerable numbers of young Latino guys who shopped there or just hung around, sometimes harassing the Asians.

"We can't be seen to know each other when we get there. During the next four hours, you try to find out whatever you can from a few of the Latino fellows hanging around the mall. I'll be available if needed, but in the background. Just don't arouse suspicion, keep it loose."

Dressed casually in jeans, a Western shirt, cowboy boots, and a belt with a large buckle, he appeared to fit the stereotype of an *immigré* Mexican national.

Jorgé took off looking into some shop windows until he saw a twenty-something young man wearing a straw sombrero. *This looks like an immigrant from Mexico*, he thought to himself, considering that it would be easier to talk with an immigrant than a local guy who might pick up on his different accent.

"*Hola*, amigo. *Como le va?*" Jorgé greeted him, smiling. "Are jou from here? Me, I'm from Chicago an' jus' visiting *mi tia vieja*. She been sick so I gots to come over here an' try to help her."

"No, amigo, I come up from Monterrey, and I been here for 'bout a year now."

"I was workin' at a big hacienda near Campeche. But there is no money down there, so me an' mi wife come to US about five or six months ago. This seem like nice place too. People so friendly. *Es lastima*, but I have to go back to Chicago in a couple a days," Jorgé rambled on ingratiatingly. "So I kind of lookin' for some good stuff here, like ganja or, well, jou know. Maybe somethin' to bet on too. That would be real good."

His new acquaintance thought about it for a minute. "Well, amigo, I do know a few guys who maybe help jou. Mi amigo Julio is someplace aroun' here, and if find heem, I tell heem to meet jou, okay?" He walked away while looking around for his friend. A few minutes later, he returned with two young Latino men and introduced Jorgé to them though he didn't know his name.

"So what kinda stuff jou looking for, amigo? Maybe some drogs or a woman, or maybe jou like a good dog fight, no?"

The two new guys were wary of anyone they didn't know. They asked a few questions of Jorgé and could tell that some of his answers didn't add up.

"Let's go have some *cerveza*, amigo. Then we can tell jou how to get some stuff. Whatever jou want, okay?"

Somewhat cautiously, Jorgé followed them toward a bar down an alley. Rambar had been watching as he sat on a bench with two elderly Asian men. He excused himself when he saw Jorgé heading away accompanied with the three men. As they turned into the alley, he went around to the far end and spotted them stopped midpoint.

"Man, I don't think jou are jus' looking for some action. I think jou are with th' *migra* or maybe the *policia*, aren't jou, huh?" one of them asked him accusingly while grabbing Jorgé's arm. The second man took hold of his other arm and started patting him down for a gun or *a wire*. Fortunately, he wasn't armed or wearing any listening device.

"I still think jou are not what jou say jou are, amigo. Somethin' is not right here, y'know," the first man said, still holding onto him.

His friend grabbed Jorgé's crotch roughly. "Maybe jou tell us jus' who jou are now, no?"

The Mexican man whom Jorgé had first approached decided this was going down way too *heavy* for him. He backed up a few steps, turned, and disappeared back down the alley. Hurting now from the grasp on his *junk*, Jorgé let out a yell.

Rambar hurried into the alley and yelled, "Hold it right there."

Both men let Jorgé go and turned to where they'd heard the shout coming from. Then they saw Rambar making a slow approach, and they started laughing at an old man confronting them.

"I'm not joking, you piece of shit. Let him go now," he said as he pulled out his weapon a few steps back. "I'll blow your goddamned heads off right now, so don't try any funny stuff. Get down on the ground and stay there."

One guy had started reaching for his knife but decided against it. Jorgé pushed them both away and joined Rambar. The two Mexicans slowly got down and spread out as they'd done before with the police. He and Jorgé quickly backed out of the alley. With their cover essentially gone, they got to their car and drove away from the Far East Center, checking to be sure they weren't followed.

"Well, that was *some* exercise, wasn't it?" Rambar said as he caught his breath.

Jorgé looked embarrassed. "I'm so sorry about this, Mr. Rambar. I didn't mean to let my guard down. I really didn't."

"Don't worry about it, Jorgé. You did all right and managed to get close to them. You were just outnumbered, that's all. Anyway, it's good training, but remember to always try to avoid going anywhere with people we don't know. It usually comes out better if you refuse to while you're in a public place with a lot of activity around. I wish we could have gotten some pictures though. Oh well."

CHAPTER 24

Rookie in Drag

Back at the office, Larry explained to Rambar that he came to Denver just to be his handler. Before heading back to Langley, he decided to discuss something with him.

"Normally the agency doesn't like sending out rookie operatives on actual assignments, as you know. However, we have a unique window of opportunity to possibly gain some important intelligence from an Iranian woman before she leaves the country. We're coordinating this action with the FBI since it's a partly domestic matter, but it's also international as well.

"Maybe you picked up that your trainee David is not a fan of the feminine gender. He's gay. More than that, he likes to dress in *drag* sometimes. This is a somewhat unusual attribute that caused our agency to recruit him in the first place. His thin build and slightly fey demeanor make him perfect for this assignment we are planning.

"Would it be a problem for you to work with him now that you are aware of that characteristic? You know that our government abandoned that bigoted area of discrimination decades ago. We found out that other qualified people could add new talents and abilities in national security matters. There was no reason to exclude gay or lesbian people from Federal employment."

"Well, if he doesn't mind that I prefer women, it's fine with me. David is a highly intelligent young man. Coming from a Middle Eastern background, he speaks both Farsi and Arabic. I don't know just how well he does, but any capability could be very useful. His name is David Ahmed al Ristoli, isn't it? I'm terrible with names, even worse now that I've gotten older."

"Because David knows and trusts you, he'd feel more comfortable on his first real assignment if you were there. Naturally this will more than count as his field exercise too."

"So this means a quick trip to DC for Edmund, doesn't it?" Rambar joked.

"Yeah, it does, old buddy, if you're willing to nursemaid your last trainee just a little while longer. What do you think?"

"If all I have to do is a quick trip to DC and watch David while he sidles up to the Iranian woman, what could possibly go wrong?" Rambar replied with a bit of sarcasm. "Well, okay, I'll do it because I'm an old fool, and I just hate to give up the *game*."

* * *

Getting into the airport VIP lounge had been arranged by the local CIA office. At 7:15 a.m., David walked into it dressed in full Muslim modesty showing only his eyes.

"Do pardon me, but would you happen to have any hand lotion? My hands feel so dry today," he asked demurely.

Looking over and apparently seeing another Muslim woman, she reached for her purse and took out a bottle of expensive hand cream.

"Oh, thank you so very much. Allah be praised. Are you going to London too?" David said softly, speaking in Farsi.

"Yes. My husband is a diplomat here, but I'm going back to Tehran soon. I want to do some shopping at Harrods in London. They are the very best department store in the world, and there are so many things that are difficult to find at home."

"Indeed, I do understand. My husband is a diplomat as well. Perhaps you would allow me to sit with you during the flight. It gets so very boring with no one to talk with on these long trips," David replied casually. His Jasmine-scented perfume wafted gently toward his new acquaintance, reassuring her that all was well.

David excused himself and headed toward the women's room, looking at his mentor as he passed by. Rambar waited a few moments then walked, limping, toward the drinking fountain near the toilets.

Paused there for a drink, David saw him stoop down to the water and whispered, "I've told the woman that I'm also on the London flight, and I need a pretext of some kind to not get on that plane."

Rambar nodded. "I'll arrange a phone call for you. Don't worry, you won't have to go to the UK right now. You don't even have your passport with you."

David returned to his seat near the Iranian woman. Rambar waited a respectable amount of time and then picked up a magazine and sat down at a distance. The flight was still nearly an hour off as David, now introduced as Najiri, made small talk near her.

"It must be so difficult for your husband with so many things going on in the world these days. These treacherous Americans make it hard for all Muslim countries to have an equal place of respect, do they not?"

"That is so very true, and Iran must be assured of our own security too, but we are prepared. Even now, my husband is coordinating with our embassy to confound these Western devils." She hesitated, thinking that perhaps she had said too much. But then, certain that this Muslim woman of great modesty would be trustworthy, she continued, "We can do great damage to them by controlling the Strait of Hormuz. Soon, our warships will threaten any shipping trying to pass through it, even firing a few warnings if necessary. Praise Allah for our great strength and determination. Oh, but dear Najiri, you must be discreet and not tell anyone about this. Can I rely on your silence?"

"Do not have a moment of concern. I shall be silent as the Great Sphinx. Do not fear. Allah will be with your devout country," David assured her sincerely.

At that moment, an attendant walked toward them. "Please excuse me, but are you Najiri Al Salman Hussaini? There is a phone call for you at the desk. Please come with me."

"That is most strange. Why does the caller not contact me on my cell phone?" David said with feigned surprise. Then looking in his purse, he said, "Oh my goodness. I seem to have misplaced it. This is most distressing. I will return momentarily."

He hurried after the attendant and picked up the phone at her desk, speaking loudly enough for the Iranian woman to hear, "But I am about to leave. Are you certain that I must? No, I don't have my cell phone at this moment. I have somehow lost it. Yes, yes, very well. I will be there as soon as possible."

He walked slowly back to the Iranian woman, his eyes appearing to look despondent. "This is terrible, but I must return to the embassy. My husband has fallen and badly injured his leg. I so looked forward to visiting with you. I am so sorry." Leaving his magazine on the chair, he hurried off.

In a short while, Rambar caught up with David on the main concourse. David ducked into the men's room and quickly shed his burka for his male clothes underneath.

"Splendid, David. That was an Oscar-winning performance. Did you learn anything worthwhile from her?"

"Yes, I think I did. We should get out of here now, shouldn't we? I'll tell you what I picked up on the way back to headquarters."

* * *

David wrote up a report on what he'd learned, and then they flew back to Denver. Once back there, David joined the other trainee operatives in a conference room. Rambar followed him in and greeted everyone.

"It has really been a genuine pleasure being with you for the past few weeks. I've learned many things from all of you, and hopefully, you have picked up a few tricks of the trade from me. You have shown your ability to adapt quickly to changing situations, to improvise, and to think fast when you need to. I'll miss working with you, but who knows what the future may hold? Now where are each of you assigned for your first duty station?"

"I'll be right here in Denver, Mr. Rambar, and maybe we will see each other again one of these days," Chanthini told him respectfully.

"Looks like I'm off to New York, sir," Jared told everyone.

Derek stated he was to going to the Anchorage Field Office.

Then Malcolm said, "I'm off to London."

Jorgé told everyone, "I'm going to be in Phoenix. Maybe I'll get to use my Spanish more if I'm in Latino countries."

Smiling broadly, David announced, "I'm being assigned to San Francisco."

They all agreed that it would be the perfect assignment for him. Worldwide duties could send them anywhere, of course, since most clandestine CIA work was done in other countries.

The next morning, Rambar flew back to Cheyenne from Denver to pick his car at that small airport. Forgetting to put his luggage in the trunk, he opened the door and noticed a note on the front passenger's seat. He unfolded it, then it struck him.

He pulled his head out of the car as quickly as he was able and limped away from the vehicle, grabbing up his bag as he went. Years of experience told him this was suspicious. A note left by anyone inside a locked car meant danger. Five seconds later, his older model Buick exploded in a huge fireball. He had just barely managed to hide behind a concrete barrier. The wide debris field scattered all around him, one small piece of metal tearing open his suitcase.

Moments later, he heard a police siren wailing in the distance. He opened the note. It read, "Goodbye, Edvard. We got your plate number in parking ramp and found you. No more you bother me, you son of a bitch. Now you go to hell, and I hoping your damn dog is with you." It was signed with "V."

"Hm," Rambar mused. "He must have seen that movie called *The Mechanic* with Charles Bronson. Really kind of stupid, Viktor. Everybody saw that film."

After the police took his statement, he brushed himself off and limped over to the terminal building to rent a car. He arrived back home in the early evening then called Loretta. She was relieved to hear his voice because he's failed to keep her notified when he'd return. He walked over to her place and saw Hunter running out to meet him.

The dog was overly excited, sensing that something had endangered his master. He jumped around and leaped up on Rambar, licking his face furiously and yelping.

Loretta came out smiling and hugged him with real affection. "I was worried about you, you old goat. Why didn't you call and let me know you were coming back today?"

As they walked into her house, she noticed that he was driving a different vehicle. "Did you trade in your old car, Edmund? Did it break down or something?"

"No, it just sort of blew up, so I rented this one. I'm going to rest for a while, Loretta. It's been a really long day."

CHAPTER 25

Rambar's Son Visits

Thinking about what type of car he should buy as a replacement, Rambar heard his house phone ring. It was Bob, his son.

"Hi, Dad, I'm already in Denver. Got here earlier than I'd planned but have a couple days of work yet. Would it be okay to drive up and see you there instead of down here? I know we'd thought about meeting in Denver."

"Oh, hello, Bob. Yes, come on up, but meet me in Cheyenne instead. That'll work out better. I need to get a different car and return this rental down there. You can pick me up at the rental agency. Then we can find me a new vehicle. Just let me know when you'll be there, all right? Good, the day after tomorrow, a Wednesday, right?"

"Yeah, Dad. I'll call you when I leave Denver. Let's have some lunch and catch up, then I'll drive you around to some car dealers. I'd still like to come up to your house anyway and meet your new *love interest*, okay?"

"That would be great, son. It's Loretta, but I'd hardly say we have a love affair going. At my age, it's more of a nice warm friendship. She'll be happy to meet you too. I've told her all about you, well, the good things anyway. You remember my dog, Hunter, don't you? I've told you that I have him, and he's a wonderful companion for me. I'll see you soon."

* * *

The weather was warm and sunny in Cheyenne. It was early April, a good car-shopping weather. Rambar and Bob visited a few dealers, and he settled on a two-year-old Chevrolet. It was a dark blue four-door model with a full warranty.

Once they got back to Rambar's house, Bob handed him an envelope. "Here's a down payment on the $70,000 you loaned Sandra and me for our house. I'll try to pay you back at least that much every year."

It was $2,000.

"Thank you, son. At that rate, you should have it all paid back by the time I'm 115," he joked good-naturedly.

"Yeah, Dad, maybe even sooner, like when you turn 112."

"You're a good boy, Bob, and I love you very much."

"Sandra and I have been thinking. We'd sure like for you to move down to Phoenix with us. We have lots of room in the house, and you'd have a nice large bedroom right on the first floor. There'd be plenty of things for you to do too. There's a senior center just three blocks away and miniature golf close by. You could do some gardening around the place or just relax by our pool. Many things to take part in locally, and you'd be close to us and your grandson, Jimmy. He's a really cute little guy."

Feigning interest but he thought, *Oh my god, they want to put me out to pasture!* Pretending to try considering it, he asked, "Would there be a bathroom near my bedroom, and is there a separate outside entrance? What about a place for Hunter? I wouldn't do it without him, you know."

"Oh sure. There's a bathroom just off your bedroom, but you'd have to use the kitchen door. It might be a problem about Hunter. Sandra's allergic to dogs and cats. Maybe Loretta would take him or something."

"Let's see if I've got this straight. I'd have a bedroom in your house but no private entrance, and I'd eat most of my meals with you two. Then I'd have to give up my best friend, Hunter. You would want me to join the activities at some senior center, so I wouldn't be underfoot in your house all the time, right?"

"Well, you're not getting any younger, Dad, and we just want what's best for you. It must get awfully boring for you up here. Probably not a lot to do in a place like this, huh?"

Rambar rolled his eyes. *If he only knew what I've been up to.* "The worst part is that I'd be away from Loretta too. She's come to mean a great deal to me."

"I'm pretty sure you'd find a nice lady friend at the senior center or somewhere. Phoenix is a large city, and there are a lot of lonely widows around," Bob countered, realizing that he was losing ground in the discussion.

"Look, son, I know you mean well, but we've never really been all that close. You were only a little boy when your mother took you away to live with her in Ohio. That was when we separated for a while and only got back together after twelve years.

"You don't know much about our family either. Your paternal great-grandfather was from Italy and immigrated to the States in 1907. His name was Edouardo Rambarini. Did you know anything about that? He married an English woman from Connecticut or maybe New Hampshire.

"Their son and daughter were both educators. The son, Angelo, changed his name to Arthur Rambar because of prejudice against Italian Americans. His sister, Antonia, married a businessman from New York, a William Bertrand.

"Arthur wed an Irish immigrant girl of seventeen years of age named Colleen, and they raised a family of three, two boys and a girl. I was one of their offspring. Unfortunately, both of your grandparents are deceased by now. I'm sorry you never met them. Sadly, your mother, my beloved wife, died about fourteen years ago, and I don't keep in contact with any of her relatives any more. So you are only one-eighth of Italian ancestry. Be proud of that too."

"No, I didn't know anything about either side of our family," Bob commented.

"Did you even know which government department I worked for, and occasionally, I still do?" Rambar pressed him further.

Bob shook his head no. "I guess that we are kind of strangers, aren't we, Dad? But that doesn't mean I don't have feelings for you and worry about how you're getting along up here."

"If I were to give up everything I have here, including my home, my dog, and my friend Loretta, then come down there to live, what would you want me to contribute to the finances? I know that maintaining your large house isn't cheap, and didn't you tell me that you and Sandra belong to a country club in the suburbs?"

"Well, Sandra, I mean…we feel that since you have a good government retirement, you'd be willing to give us much of it to help out, right?"

"Okay, son. Here's the deal I'll make with you. I more than suspect that Sandra is the one behind your proposal. Knowing what your lifestyle is like, she thinks that if I move down there and contribute to the pot, you probably won't go belly-up and file bankruptcy. Am I right, son?"

"That's putting it pretty harsh, Dad. We are a bit short of ready cash right now, which is why we could only give you the $2,000. But our main reason is that we love you and want what we feel best for you."

"Actually, it's what you both *think* is best for me, isn't it? So back to my deal. I'll waive all of the remaining money you owe me, about $68,000. You won't have to pay me a cent. The debt is canceled. The condition is this: you will never propose any plan in the future to get me down there and live with you, understood?"

"I'm very happy and active here despite what you might think. It would only be a short time until Sandra and I would lock horns, and she'd want me out of there. You don't know that I overheard the two of you talking during your wedding reception. She told you, 'I don't know what we'll do when your father can't look after himself and needs to be cared for. Maybe we can put him in a nursing home, if they don't cost too much. Or worst case, maybe let him stay in our house 'til he dies.'"

"Gee, Dad, I don't know what to say. I guess this means you won't consider coming down to live in Phoenix?"

"You've got that right, Bob. I'm a long way from being feeble or addlebrained. Even if I were, Loretta is a hundred times kinder and more compassionate than your scheming wife is. And she loves Hunter as much as I do. So when you get back home, you can tell Sandra, however you want to phrase it, that I have considered it carefully and feel that I'm much better off settled here. I'm happy and have no wish to either intrude in your lives or to give you most of what money you may think I have. Is that clear enough?"

Seeing that Rambar was adamant and was right that he wouldn't get on well with Sandra, Bob nodded his head in agreement. The conversation was over permanently. His dad was a stronger personality than him. "Okay, I'll tell Sandra that you're determined to stay up here and to please not bring it up again."

Rambar could discern that his son was worried about their finances. He softened and hugged Bob. "Look, son, I know it's very hard to keep everything afloat financially these days. I'll give you $4,000 to help out. It won't cut me short of cash and would maybe satisfy Sandra somewhat. Now let's go and see Loretta, okay?"

"To be honest, Dad, I really need to get back to Denver and finish some stuff up. Please tell Loretta that I'm sorry and that I'll meet her some other time, okay? I'll take off in a few minutes, but I do hate to leave so soon."

"Sure, son, I understand. We'll get together again one of these days."

As soon as Bob left, Rambar and Hunter headed over to Loretta's. On arriving, he grabbed her and hugged her. "You mean so much to me, Loretta, even more than I'd realized. I love you so very much." He had a few tears in his eyes but kept hugging her so she wouldn't see him crying. "Would you make this old man happier than he's been in many years? Please marry me."

"Edmund, I'm so glad you're back, and I love you too. I'd hoped that you would propose to me. Of course, I will, a thousand times yes. Is your son coming over? I'd love to meet him."

"No, he took off already saying he had to get back to finish up some last-minute work in Denver. The truth is, though, when I wouldn't agree to move down to Phoenix and live with them, he just wanted to leave. I'm pretty sure it was all his wife's idea to get some more money to support their lifestyle.

"Anyway, I told him that I'm happy here and not to bother me with that stupid idea again. He even said that I couldn't bring Hunter down there with me. His wife, Sandra, is allergic to dogs. I didn't even consider it at all, but that was the clincher. I did buy a different car while we were in Cheyenne. You'll have to look at it, and we can go for a drive. Hunter hasn't been in it yet either, and he'll need to approve it, of course."

CHAPTER 26

Planning a Vacation

Later, after having a light supper, they went for a drive in the Chevy with Hunter happily nestled into the back seat.

"I'm tired, and it would be nice to take a vacation and get away for a while. What would you think about that, dear heart?" Edmund asked Loretta, looking over her way affectionately.

"Well, I've always had this dream of taking an ocean cruise to somewhere exotic. Unlike you, I haven't traveled very much, only down to Mexico a couple of times. How does that sound, or do you get seasick?"

"No, that could be very relaxing. Mostly, I've traveled by plane because I had to get there fast." Then thinking to himself, *Or get out of somewhere fast.*

"It wouldn't matter where, just so we could be together and have Hunter along with us," she mused. "Those ships allow animals, don't they?"

"We can find out for sure. Can you look it up on your computer, Loretta? I don't know a damned thing about how to work 'em. Don't think I could even turn one on."

"Of course. We'll check it out when we get back to the house, dear Edmund," she said, gently touching his arm reassuringly.

After more than an hour on her computer, they discovered that few, if any, large cruise ships accepted pets aboard their excursions. Even companion animals for the blind were discouraged.

"Now here's a possibility, Edmund. Some of the freighters that also take passengers will allow dogs too. That might be the answer. If they won't take Hunter along, then a cruise is out. It seems like the foreign cargo ships are more interested in travelers with pets than American-based ones. Let me look under *foreign cargo/passenger carriers*."

Loretta carefully scanned a listing of possible freight liners. "Here are some Greek ships that take up to twenty-eight passengers and accept dogs. They even have a doggie play area with sand for them."

"Well, that sounds promising. Does it say where they go?" Edmund asked, interested. "Do you get seasick?"

"No. It doesn't say where they go, only that their ports of call, as they put it, vary depending on where their cargo need to go. Some of their ships come to the States. I think I'm okay on the water. When I was a teenager, my folks took me across Lake Michigan from Milwaukee to somewhere in Michigan and I was fine."

"Let's drive down to Cheyenne and talk with a travel agent about it. They'll have more detailed information and maybe some brochures," Edmund offered. Loretta nodded in agreement.

Two days later, they were seated with a woman at the American Express office.

"The ship we found for you folks sounds ideal. It's called *The Pericles*, and they have a good itinerary," she offered.

"You are certain they take pets, aren't you?" Loretta asked.

"Yes, they definitely do, up to five animals on each cruise, dogs or cats. *The Pericles* has a somewhat regular schedule. They normally stop at Istanbul, Piraeus and Crete in Greece, Naples, Nice, Barcelona, Lisbon, Canary Islands, then to the US at Biloxi, Mississippi."

"I'm in for it. What do you think, Loretta?" Edmund asked, sounding very enthusiastic. "Do you have a passport?"

"Let's do it, Edmund. 'I'd like to get you on a slow boat to China,' like that old song says, but this will be fine."

They hugged and kissed each other.

"I do have a passport that I've never used but got it hoping that someday…"

* * *

Back at home the next day, Rambar was packing clothes for the trip when he heard Hunter bark. The phone was ringing downstairs. He'd left it on the kitchen table and hurried there to pick it up.

"Hi, Edmund. Larry here. I heard on the grapevine that your car got blown to smithereens in Cheyenne. The local police there contacted our office and the FBI for technical assistance on the case. So Borenko was up to his old tricks again, eh."

"Yeah, it was him. As you probably heard, he left me a little love note signed with a big V at the bottom. By now, I'm sure he's out of the country and probably laughing about it in Moscow, thinking he finally got me."

"Well, screw him again. None of the agencies contacted the Russians about it. So as far as they know, you're a dead issue." Larry chuckled. "What are you planning on next?"

"My girlfriend Loretta and I are going on a cruise over to Europe in a week or so. This is still a secure line, isn't it, Larry?"

"Hell yes, it's the same phone I gave you before you took off for London, remember?"

"Yes, now that you've refreshed my memory. I'd completely for-gotten about it. We're going on a passenger-carrying freighter because they allow dogs. Can't leave Hunter out of the action. He's our best friend and *fur baby*, as other pet lovers say."

"That's great. You deserve a good vacation after all you went through. What ship are you and Loretta going on?" Larry asked.

"It's…um… *The Pericles*, and it docks at Biloxi. We'll pick it up there, and its first stop is the Canary Islands. I think I'll buy Loretta a couple of canaries," Edmund joked.

"Hm, that kind of rings a bell. Let me check on the computer, okay? It won't take long. Ah yes, here it is, *The Pericles*. We like to keep an eye on some of these freighters just to see what they're up to. How would you like to do us a favor and casually observe anything

116

shady that might be going on? It wouldn't involve you taking any action, but if you happen to see something…"

"Oh boy, here we go again, right?" Rambar feigned lamenting. "Can't I just be left alone to take a nice vacation with my girlfriend?"

"Sure, Edmund, no pressure. Only if you want to help us out. By some strange coincidence, we happen to have one of our planes heading to New Orleans about that time. We could give you folks a lift and drop you off in Biloxi, no problem. That way, Hunter would be in the cabin with you and not in a crate down in the baggage compartment. But no pressure," Larry cajoled him.

"Okay, okay, I'll keep my eyes open but no promises. They may be completely above board, but if not, I'll call you about what I find. By the way, does the agency have return flights back from New Orleans sometime as well?"

"You do drive a hard bargain, you old skinflint. We'll arrange something."

After explaining to Loretta that an old friend from his agency was doing them a favor, they boarded an inconspicuous plane at Denver International. It was a De Havilland Dash 8 parked outside on one of the smaller hangers at the edge of the airfield. There were two other passengers on board, both CIA operatives.

Hunter, with a seat belt around him, looked out the window unruffled. Being a slower aircraft, the flight took just under four hours, without much turbulence. They took a taxi to a hotel near the waterfront and settled in until the next morning.

CHAPTER 27

Aboard a Freighter

Aboard *The Pericles*, they watched the harbor slowly disappear as their adventure began. Among the twenty or so people standing by the railing on the port side was an attractive woman in her fifties, expensively dressed. Her companion was a standard poodle, light grey, almost pink in color.

"Does that woman look familiar to you, Edmund? I could swear that I saw her somewhere a long time ago."

Edmund replied politely but not recognizing the woman either. At that moment, Hunter noticed the beautiful poodle. Still on his long leash, he slowly ambled over toward the strangely attractive dog and gently sniffed her. He knew it was a female even before the sniff test.

She turned to him, her tail wagging happily. Hunter was doing the same, tail flopping in excitement.

The woman saw Hunter and cautioned her dog. "You be careful now, Princess. He may not like you," she said, realizing quickly that this was not just another friendly female.

Hunter looked up at her, perhaps thinking, *What are you talking about, lady? I love this cutie. She's beautiful.*

"It's all right, Princess. He seems to like you, so be nice to him. He's a beautiful boy." She reached down to pet him and Hunter knew he was *in*.

Loretta went over to the woman. "Oh, I hope our dog isn't bothering you or your beautiful poodle. Did I hear you call her Princess?"

"Yes, she truly is a princess, and our dogs are getting on well together, aren't they? What is the name of this handsome creature?"

"This is Hunter, and my name is Loretta. This is Edmund," she said as he joined them. "You look so familiar. Is it possible that I know you from somewhere?"

"Perhaps you remember me from some film or other that I was in. God only knows how long ago that was. My name is Wanda Wendover, and I'm so pleased to meet you."

"This will be our first time on a cruise, and we're really looking forward to it. Edmund has been in Europe before, but I never have, so it will really be an adventure. It's also our first trip together," Loretta bubbled on happily.

"Hello, Ms. Wendover. I used to travel in Europe quite often— on business," Edmund said briefly. He had learned over the years to not divulge too much information at first. Anyone could possibly be doing something of interest to the agency, even this friendly woman.

Later, they would have dinner together and talk more. With so few passengers, everyone could dine at the captain's table if they wished.

The other passengers were a diverse lot. There was a young couple, likely on their honeymoon. Then a few Middle Eastern people, apparently all traveling together, who kept to themselves. A wealthy-looking Mexican couple were traveling with the mother in one of them. A mature English couple were easily identified by their accent. Of the others aboard, not much could be determined.

Edmund had noticed the English ones up on deck, but they were farther down the railing. He thought the man looked familiar. After dinner, a few of the men wandered topside for a smoke or just fresh air. Closer now to the Englishman, Edmund realized who he was. He quietly approached and asked, "You're Nigel, aren't you? I'm Edmund Rambar, AC4YN."

"Ah, yes. Lhasa, Tibet, but I remember you as Lord Chesterton-Rancourt. You are traveling with a lovely lady, are you not?"

"Yes, my fiancée, Loretta. Rambar is my real name, and I'm traveling on my diplomatic passport. Now how about you, Nigel?"

"I shall have to get used to calling you Edmund. I'm on holiday with my wife, Dorris, with two *r*s. I'm also keeping an eye open for any illicit activity. Probably safer if we appear to have just met, don't you think, old boy?" Nigel replied, still speaking softly.

"Agreed, I'm doing the same as you." He then started speaking much louder for the benefit of any listeners close by. "I'm very happy to make your acquaintance. My name is Edmund Rambar. You'll have to meet Loretta a bit later."

"Delighted as well. I am Nigel Brown, and you must meet my dear wife."

Over dinner, the ladies, including Wanda, get better acquainted and chatter animatedly about the dogs, about where everyone is from, and what to wear in the various countries.

Appearing to be new friends, Nigel and Edmund have a drink at the small bar and are greeted by the ship's captain, Miklos Demetriopoulos. He seems to be a straight shooter and quite competent. Working around the salon, he left shortly to welcome other passengers to his ship.

Speaking quietly again, Nigel commented, "A good bit of luck meeting you here. We can work together again. After all, two heads are better than one, old boy."

"Well, yes, except, perhaps, not on the same body," Rambar replied, joking.

* * *

While the ladies explored and shopped at the first few ports, Nigel and Edmund explored the ship. At their request, Captain Demetriopoulos told the first officer to give them the full tour. They admired the engines, controls on the bridge, and the ample lifeboats on deck.

Less obviously, they carefully took note of certain crates in the storage hold. When the first officer was momentarily called up to the bridge, Nigel observed that one of the crates near them was not properly sealed. Rambar found a crowbar, and they pried open the lid.

Inside, packed under the straw, they found an assortment of weapons: AK-47s, Uzis, and older American-made guns.

"It looks like somebody's ordered a bargain-basement assortment of cheap weapons to play with, doesn't it, Nigel?"

"Yes, I think you're right, Edmund. They're going to some rebel group or other that doesn't have a lot of cash to spend. Now if we can find out where."

They checked the markings on several of the similar-looking crates and wrote them down on Edmund's small notepad. Each one was stenciled "Farm Tools" or "Tractor Parts." Inside the one they pried open, Nigel found a bill of lading, which he quickly pocketed. They resealed the opened crate.

The first officer returned and offered to show them the radio room. They made a show of interest as they proceeded.

Inside, Rambar asked, "Do you still use ICW [International Morse Code] at all these days, or am I completely out of date?"

Answering politely, the first officer told him, "No, it's all by voice communication these days, sir." He thought to himself, *This guy's really a dinosaur—Morse Code, really.*

They both offered their appreciation and returned to Nigel's cabin. They checked out the bill of lading he took. Not listing weapons at all, the items shown were farm tools and tractor parts. What most interest both men was the final destination, Somalia via Libya and off-loading at the port of Tripoli.

"Interesting, isn't it? A somewhat circuitous route to Somalia. Still, unloading falsely marked crates in a passably stable place like Libya avoids suspicion."

"With a bribe or two in the right hands...well," Edmund deduced.

"It's a lengthy land route but taking them through Libya and Sudan is probably safer," Nigel considered. "They might also take them to some port in Sudan, then by water down to the Somali coast. Who knows for sure?"

"In any case, we know that there will be an unscheduled stop in Libya. When they unload the crates, we must get an accurate count of how many there are and, if possible, who's going to transport them. Then we'll contact MI6 and the CIA with what we have," Nigel stated, looking at Edmund who concurred.

* * *

The women joyfully browsed in the shops along Las Ramblas in Barcelona. Returning to their respective cabins, each laid out treasures they'd found for their mates' approval.

"Edmund, I bought you a little gift," Loretta announced happily and handed Edmund a box containing two new shirts.

He opened it and looked very pleased, then hugged her and gave her a big kiss. "This is so wonderful, dear heart. I forgot to pack enough dress shirts. You are so thoughtful, and they're beautiful."

She smiled back, giving him a peck on the cheek, pleased that he liked her gift. "I'm so tired from all the running around. We went to the Picasso Museum and even saw a flamenco dance performance right out on some plaza. It was wonderful, Edmund. I'm so glad we came on this trip."

* * *

After cruising through the night, the ship docked in Nice, France. Most of the ladies decided to have an onshore lunch at one of the elegant old hotels, then go shopping. The vessel would remain in port until late evening.

Nigel and Edmund decided to pay a visit to Inspector Gerard in Monte Carlo, only a few miles distant, in Monaco. Edmund phoned ahead and spoke with the police official. He was delighted to hear from, as he believed, Lord Chesterton-Rancourt. He had spoken with Nigel by phone before Edmund's first visit, a few weeks earlier.

They chose to go by Heli Air Monaco and arrived at the chopper port just before 11:00 a.m. Taking a taxi, they arrived shortly at the police headquarters. Inspector Gerard greeted them warmly and suggested having lunch at the nearby Hôtel Hermitage.

He was pleased to meet Nigel in person and referred to Edmund as Lord Rancourt. They saw no need to inform Gerard of his real name or that he was, in fact, an American. Thus, Edmund spoke with his British accent when they again met.

"Ah, Lord Rancourt, or do you prefer Edmund Rambar?" Gerard asked casually.

Both Edmund and Nigel were caught off guard and embarrassed. How did this police Inspector know Edmund's true identity?

"Please understand that we were not attempting to deceive you, Inspector, but since you had begun using Edmund's operational identity, we thought it better to not contradict you. Do forgive us," Nigel admitted sheepishly.

"Oh, do not feel at all uncomfortable about it, Nigel. In this business, no one uses their real name, do they? We do take some degree of pride in knowing many things about our friends, as well as our adversaries," Gerard offered soothingly, with a pleased smile at his *coup*.

"Thank you for being so gracious, Inspector, and a sincere toast to the Monegasque Police Department," Edmund said, raising his glass of cognac.

They explained they were on a vacation cruise with their ladies and wanted to pay a visit to the principality and to Gerard. It was Nigel's first visit, and he hoped to do some sightseeing during their time here.

"I'm told that the Exotic Gardens are most interesting, and the casino is a must for me," Nigel said enthusiastically.

"Since I've been here before, I'm eager to show him around your beautiful country," Edmund offered. "We really must take a walk through the Princess Grace Rose Garden. The flowers and statuary are quite excellent."

"Where is your next port of call?" Inspector Gerard asked with interest.

"Our itinerary shows a stop in Naples. However, we have reason to believe that there will be a detour into Tripoli. Some of the cargo is being off-loaded there, and we suspect an illegal shipment of weapons is involved," Nigel explained.

"If that is true, please contact me should some assistance be required," Gerard told them.

CHAPTER 28

Pirate Attack

"What a beautiful little country, Monaco," Nigel exclaimed. "To think that such a small place has so much coastline and an amazing number of yachts docked there. I really want to take Dorris there some time."

"Yes, it's a little jewel. Inspector Gerard is fine man too. I think that most Monegasques are extremely friendly people," Edmund agreed.

* * *

As *The Pericles* steamed out of the Nice harbor, the wives told the men about their adventures there. Wanda Wendover had set her sights on the good-looking young men along the beaches and the waiters in the hotels. The other women quickly realized that she was a genuine *cougar*.

"Nigel, I meant to tell you about a new CIA operative who will be stationed in London quite soon. He's one of several rookies to whom I taught a course on *deception and evasion* just before we came on this cruise. His name is Malcolm Donahue, and he's a highly intelligent young man. I believe he'll go far in the organization when he gains some experience."

"I look forward to meeting him, and since your agency's office in London is relatively small, I undoubtedly will in time."

The afternoon passed slowly after a pleasant lunch on the aft deck. Edmund and Nigel stopped along the railing to exchange work-related stories. The ship was closing in on Tripoli, about twenty miles distant, when they noticed two high-speed motor cruisers heading toward their ship. As they came within distance, there were several men on each one armed with machine guns.

"What the heck are those people, pirates?" Rambar exclaimed with some concern. "I didn't think there were any in the Mediterranean."

"Really, I haven't the foggiest," Nigel said, completely mystified. "They can't be customs or a harbor pilot, and there are no markings on the boats."

Some of the men in the boats began firing their weapons into the air, shouting in Arabic. A few moments later, Captain Demetriopoulos began talking on the ship's speakers.

"Your attention everyone. This is your captain speaking. Do not be alarmed, but we are likely to be boarded by possible hijackers. There is no way by which we can outmaneuver them with this vessel. Return to your cabins immediately and lock yourselves in. If they come onboard, we will do everything within our capability to ensure the safety of all passengers," he announced first in English, then in Greek.

Shortly after, the two boats came alongside and secured to the ship. Most of the unidentified men clambered up the exterior stairways on both sides, brandishing their weapons.

Captain Demetriopoulos bravely met them on the main deck. "What is it you want from our ship?" he asked in a confident voice. He was used to being in command.

"Open the cargo hatches, NOW," the apparent leader of the gang shouted, waving his machine gun menacingly.

The captain motioned for his men to comply. They unsecured both main hatches, then awaited further orders. Two of the intruders jumped down onto nearby crates below and began checking the markings. They seemed to be looking for something specific.

Soon, they shouted something to their leader about moving a cargo crane into place. Complying rapidly, the ship's crew moved it into proper position. The two men below were joined by two more from the deck. All of the remaining hijackers held crew members hostage while the below-deck activity was taking place.

"We do not want hurt anybody, so do what we say, you understand?" the leader warned the crew and captain, speaking in broken English.

"We do not wish any trouble," Captain Demetriopoulos replied, nodding.

The same crates Nigel and Edmund had identified were now being off-loaded onto the smaller boats alongside. Both men had returned to their respective cabins to be with their wives but watched the proceedings from the portholes. Hunter lay uneasily on the floor next to Princess, realizing that something was wrong.

Within the next half hour, fifty-two crates, by Edmund's count, had been reloaded onto the two boats.

"We want food now, hot stuff. You get for us, then we leave, no problem," their leader shouted to the captain. Grabbing the hastily prepared meal, they departed.

Earlier, Wanda had brought Princess to Loretta and Edmund's cabin to be with Hunter. Then Rambar and Nigel opened the door to their adjoining compartments and began analyzing the situation.

"Interesting that they didn't rob the passengers," Nigel said. "They knew what they were looking for and took only those crates."

"Somebody on board had to tip them off as to which ship they were on or maybe one of the passengers using a cell phone. That is, if they knew that the crates were on-board," Edmund surmised.

Loretta and Dorris were eagerly taking all of this in. Relieved that the hijackers had departed, they began piecing it all together.

"Did either of you two know what was in those crates?" Loretta asked.

"Well, yes. We did some snooping around on the ship. It's an occupational hazard, I suppose. Just can't get it out of your blood after doing it for so long," Edmund replied. "It was guns."

"Obviously, the hijackers weren't the ones that the guns were meant for, so they had to grab them before the ship reached Tripoli, right? They must have left some type of clues, didn't they? I've read a lot of spy and mystery novels, and there are always a few clues," Loretta continued.

"Yes, you're right, Loretta. Let's see what we do know right now. Who would be most likely to benefit with the least risk? What do you think, Nigel?" Edmund asked, turning to him.

"The two boats used by the hijackers were not marked, but we can describe them by color, approximate length, etc. We can describe the leader and some of the men with him though we'll probably never see any of them again. Only the leader had any really distinctive features, a gold upper tooth right in the front of his mouth. He also had a large green dragon tattoo on his left forearm," Nigel recalled.

"What about notifying the authorities when we get into port?" Dorris inquired.

"Yes, good point. I feel that we should identify ourselves to the captain and let him know what we know. My experience tells me that he is completely trustworthy. He would be risking his career by being a part to any conspiracy. Remember he told us that he'd worked for this shipping company for over thirty-six years and had only a short time before retiring," Nigel stated confidently.

The two men walked up to the bridge and met with Captain Demetriopoulos.

"We will be docking very soon, and I am most happy that you have told me all this. It is good that I have two intelligence officials with me to explain what has occurred. I did not know what the crates contained except what was indicated on the markings. Thank you both so much," he exclaimed gratefully.

"Fortunately, we were able to take the bill of lading from one of the crates when your first officer gave us the tour," Nigel said as he handed it to the captain.

"Excellent, gentlemen, you have been more than helpful," he again thanked them. "Oh, I almost forgot. My cook was most resourceful. He put some rat poison into the lunch we provided to the hijackers. The maritime authorities in port have only to look for some very sick sailors, do they not?" he said, smiling.

The next morning, after several hours of speaking with the local authorities, the captain was given leave to depart, and the ship was again underway. He had a big decision to make. If he backtracked to unload freight in Naples, it would add nearly a thousand extra miles to the voyage.

After conferring with the vessel's home office, he ordered that *The Pericles* then stop in Naples on the return trip. This would arouse the ire of companies expecting their cargo to arrive by a certain date but was unavoidable.

Upon arriving in Crete and disembarking, the party of five, including Edmund, Nigel, and the three women, decided to explore the island. After several hours of sightseeing in the uncomfortably warm sun, they stopped at a hotel restaurant for a late afternoon lunch and drinks. Wanda wistfully eyed three young Greek navy officers at a nearby table. Dorris and Loretta showed the men their purchases. Edmund commented that it had been better to leave the dogs onboard instead of having them out in the hot weather and everyone agreed.

As they were finishing lunch, Nigel's cell phone rang. It was Captain Demetriopoulos with news about the hijacking. Five men had been admitted to a Libyan hospital with symptoms of stomach distress. An "alert notification" by the authorities about suspicious cases requiring medical care had resulted in the hospital calling them.

Using their *gentle* techniques of persuasion, which police in Arab countries are so well known for, they elicited confessions from two of the suspects. After arriving on shore at a remote beach east of the city, the crates of weapons had been loaded onto trucks marked *Atlas International Transport Company*.

During interrogation by both the captain and local authorities, Niklos, the full-time radio man on the ship, realized that he had been relieved by his alternate. This was a cargo handler named Stavros, who also filled in as an alternate radio operator, and had offered to let Niklos go below for dinner.

When confronted, Stavros eventually confessed that he had sent a message to the hijackers. Because this had occurred at sea outside the territorial waters of Libya, the captain arrested and locked him up in an improvised cell aboard ship. When the vessel put into port at Piraeus, he would be turned over to Greek authorities for trial.

Unable to obtain any further information, the police determined that the hijackers had only been hired to steal the crates and bring them ashore. The trucks and drivers were waiting for them, accompanied by an East African man. He paid the hijackers as agreed and then left with the trucks and crates, their destination still unknown.

Over six hours had elapsed since the police began interrogating all five suspects; the guns were now likely close to the borders of a number of other countries or even put onto planes and flown to Somalia. Nevertheless, the authorities issued bulletins to towns along the southern Libya borders, hoping for any information.

This provided Edmund and Nigel with sufficient intelligence to contact their respective agencies. Undercover operatives located in East Africa were subsequently provided with the information they had obtained. Their part in it was over.

Both men admitted privately to Dorris and Loretta that they were doing some general observational work for their agencies. They had been briefed that illegal weapons were being transported on cargo ships, one of which turned out to be the freighter they were on. They strongly cautioned the women not to tell anyone, even Wanda, about their activities.

"This is just like some spy novel, isn't it, Loretta?" Dorris exclaimed excitedly.

Both men looked sternly at her, again repeating their admonitions.

* * *

Arriving at Piraeus the next day, Stavros attempted to escape but was taken into custody and got jailed. Again, statements had to be made and documents filled out before *The Pericles* could continue on to Istanbul and unload more cargo.

By now, Captain Demetriopoulos, grateful for all the help by Nigel and Edmund, insisted that they and the women join him at a smaller, more private table for lunch. Because Wanda had also joined them, only small talk was made, mostly about the city of Piraeus and the sights to be seen there.

By 2:00 p.m., four of the group had set off to look over various tourist spots the captain had told them about. Demetriopoulos had business to take care of at the company headquarters and departed at the same time. Edmund decided to stay on board and play with the dogs. His knee was bothering him badly, and he'd had enough sun for a while.

After assuring the passengers that there would be time for them to visit Athens on the return visit, everyone was satisfied. At 8:00 p.m., the ship left port for a night, crossing to Istanbul, the city in both Europe and Asia.

CHAPTER 29

Saved by Loretta

Istanbul appeared even more mysterious and exotic to Loretta and Dorris than the earlier places they'd visited. Wanda had shot a movie on location there years earlier and was somewhat familiar with that city. However, she had not been feeling well and decided to rest in her cabin. Edmund felt better and wanted to see the city himself, not having ever been there before. He did take along his cane in case his right knee began acting up.

They toured the Hagia Sophia and marveled at how long it had been in existence, then the Topkapi Palace and other Ottoman Empire sites. Dorris had hoped to see Mount Ararat but learned it was too far distant for even a full day's trip. She told them that Nigel would try to join them for dinner ashore later.

After stopping for a light lunch and mint tea, they shopped in one of the covered malls. Dorris spotted some beautifully embroidered fabrics and was negotiating a price with the shopkeeper. Loretta looked at the brass pieces in another stall while Edmund was nearby getting some Turkish cigarettes.

As he was pulling a bill out of his wallet, a young man appeared out of nowhere and grabbed at it. He pushed Edmund hard against a display of small rugs, and he dropped his cane.

It caught him by surprise, and the assailant grabbed the whole billfold while turning to run away. Loretta, meaning to show some object to Edmund, saw what was happening and forcefully swung the brass bookend at the thief. He shrieked, dropped Edmund's wallet, and fled, rubbing his wounded face.

Recovering his footing, Edmund smiled gratefully and hugged Loretta. "Why, Loretta dear, you're not just another pretty face. I should have had you as my partner on the job. You saved my wallet, and I love you," he said as he kissed her.

"Oh, you're just an old geezer, and I can see that I'm going to have to take care of you. After all, I am about twenty years younger than you are," she gently teased him.

Seeing the commotion, Dorris hurried over to them. "Oh, I do wish Nigel were here to help," she uttered excitedly.

"It's all right, Dorris. Loretta handled the problem quite well. The thief gained nothing for his attempt except possibly a broken nose," Edmund replied reassuringly.

"Would you like to go back to the ship, Edmund?" Loretta asked, concerned.

"No, of course not, dear. You should probably buy that nice bookend though. It was an effective weapon and a nice souvenir too," he replied, smiling.

After an enjoyable dinner at an outdoor restaurant along the Bosporus, they returned to the ship. Edmund and Nigel decided to stroll around the deck and talk about the day's events.

"The Swiss have been developing synthetic DNA, and my agency is working on practical uses for it," Nigel began. "Apparently, it can be put inside a neutral material such as plastic and molded into any shape whatsoever."

"I'm hopelessly out of date on almost any technology. This is the first time I've ever heard about it. I barely understand just what DNA is or what the letters signify," Edmund answered with some interest. "Here's something *you* might find interesting, Nigel. The CIA, my agency, had been working on how climate change might affect our intelligence gathering around the world. In fact, we had set up a climate center to study it and gained some good information for over three years."

"Unfortunately, a few of our shortsighted members of congress cut off the funding, so we had to scrap the whole project. One of them naively commented that 'we should be monitoring terrorists in caves instead of polar bears on icebergs,'" Edmund explained with disgust.

"It is sad, isn't it?" Nigel lamented. "There are supposedly intelligent people in our parliaments or legislatures who just can't see the forest for the trees."

* * *

Back inside the salon, Captain Demetriopoulos made an announcement to the passengers who were present, having an evening cocktail. "We have been notified that we must make another change to our route and include an additional stop in Romania to take on more freight. As you know, this is on the Black Sea and will add three days to our voyage. Such is what frequently happens with cargo ships, but it may inconvenience some of our passengers.

"Therefore, if any of you need to end your trip with us at this point, our company will fly you to any European city you wish at no cost. We will also refund the balance of your ticket for any unused portion. The new Havalimani International Airport here in Istanbul serves all major cities regularly, and your reservations will include first-class seating."

There was immediate discussion among several of the passengers. The three Mexican people decided to disembark and fly back to Spain. Some of the others decided on Paris or London. Nigel and Dorris thought it over carefully. Although they regretted having to part company with Loretta and Edmund, they decided to return to Nice so Dorris could see Monte Carlo. Most of the travelers continued on the cruise, glad to pick up an extra port at no additional cost. After sailing through the Bosporus eastbound into the Black Sea, the ship hugged the coastline until reaching the port of Constanta, Romania.

Regretting the departure of their friends, Edmund, Loretta, and Wanda decided to stay close to the ship. They settled for taking the dogs on a short walk along the dock. The town appeared to offer little of interest anyway. Wanda commented that it would be fun to see

Dracula's castle, but it was too far and they weren't sure about safety concerns.

After having coffee at an outside stand, they continued walking. Suddenly something attracted the attention of Princess, Wanda's poodle. She bolted toward a workman who was coiling rope along the boards of the dock. When she got close to his leg, he kicked at her forcefully. More startled than hurt, she yelped loudly.

Hunter growled and took off at a fast run to rescue his girlfriend. The man saw him coming and swatted at the dog with a length of rope. It connected hitting Hunter across his muzzle. Then the man kept whipping him violently, striking several strong blows to his head and shoulders. Then he kicked the injured animal in the ribs. Hunter was hurt and cried out in pain.

Princess had shaken her head and was ready for action. She bit into the man's ankle, but he kicked her away, still hitting Hunter repeatedly. Edmund was up now and limped toward the fracas as quickly as he could, followed by the two women. They were about sixty or seventy feet away, yelling at the man to stop.

There was blood on Hunter's coat. Edmund saw it and lost all control. He swung his cane at the assailant, shouting, "You bastard, I'll kill you. I'm seventy-nine years old, but I swear I'll kill you!"

The man tried unsuccessfully to grab the cane, but Edmund poked at vital points staccato-like until the man dropped the rope. He tackled Edmund, and they staggered toward the edge of the dock. Loretta ran over to help as they broke free of each other. She put out her left foot behind the angry man, and Edmund managed to give him a strong push. He fell into the water nearly twelve feet below. The tide had come into the deep harbor. He sank beneath the surface, and the three above waited for him to bob up. He didn't. The dock was deserted. No one else had observed what was going on.

"Should we call the police or something?" Wanda asked in a frightened voice.

Edmund was completely out of breath but shook his head no. "This is…Romania. No one knows what the police might…do here. At the least…they'd take the dogs and…and…probably arrest us," Edmund explained. "Let's get out…of here, fast."

Loretta helped Edmund, and they all walked away quickly and headed back to the ship unnoticed. Aboard, Rambar explained the situation to the captain, whom he trusted.

"Do not be concerned, Edmund. I have no love for the corrupt authorities here. You were defending yourselves and dear Hunter."

They gently took the injured dog down to the ship's doctor who carefully examined him.

"No broken bones, but he suffered a few scrapes and bruises. In his mouth, it looks like maybe he has a piece of that fellow. I will swab out his teeth and tongue to stop any infection, do not worry. He is a good dog. Next, I will also examine Princess. She too might have a piece of that horrible man," the doctor said, half amused.

"I should also check you over too, Mr. Rambar," he added in his professional tone.

CHAPTER 30

An Informant

Back aboard, Rambar received a call on his secure phone. It was Larry in DC.

"Are you and Loretta enjoying your vacation, Edmund? We have an unbelievable opportunity while you're over there. Let me tell you about it, okay?"

"Well, I've had quite enough excitement for one day, Larry, but go ahead," Edmund replied weakly.

"We know about a group of professional hitmen, assassins, who kill anyone if they're paid enough, mainly important international figures. The trouble is that we don't have much intelligence about 'em. One of our informants lives there in Romania and can provide much needed information to us. He's a merchant seaman and works on cargo vessels in the Black Sea and the Mediterranean. If you could meet him and learn whatever he can provide, it could be a lot of good stuff for us. Can you do it, Edmund?"

"I'm willing, but here's the problem. I can't leave the ship again because something bad went down on the dock. The police might be investigating it now, but I can't be sure. Our ship is leaving port at 7:00 p.m., or sooner if the cargo is loaded. How could I meet with your informant before then?" Rambar wondered. "I'll see if Captain Demetriopoulos has any ideas."

He hurried up to the bridge and explained the situation. The skipper listened sympathetically and had a good idea.

"You know, Edmund, a ship is always short of deck hands. If this informant man has seaman's papers, I could hire him right now, and he would have time to tell you his information. Then if he wants to leave my ship in Istanbul, or wherever, it would be okay. What do you think?"

"I think you've hit upon a perfect solution, Captain. I'll call my people right now and set it up. All they have to do is get that guy aboard before we sail."

At 6:40 p.m., the gangplank was still attached to the dock, but the crew was readying the ship for departure. Edmund watched tensely for a man to appear. In a few minutes, an older nautical-looking man appeared along the dock. Seeing it was the right ship, he walked up the gangplank and identified himself to the captain, who had joined Rambar.

Demetriopoulos asked if he possessed seaman's papers and said if he did, there was an opening for a deckhand. Agreeing affirmatively, the man pulled a certificate out of his shirt pocket and handed it to the captain.

"Okay, I can use you," he told the man. "This is Mr. Rambar, and he will take you somewhere in privacy so you two can talk alone."

Retrieving his papers, the man seemed very grateful for not having to leave.

In one of the unoccupied cabins, Rambar used CIA protocols to verify the man's authenticity and truthfulness. After a series of seemingly innocuous questions, he was cautiously satisfied that the individual was telling the truth. This was further supported by the man's nervous actions. He appeared fearful for his own safety and mentioned several times that he could not return to Constanta or his job.

The years had not diminished Rambar's ability to judge between veracity and deception. He asked the man's name, which was Shazkur, and then introduced himself as Edmund. Getting into specific information, he asked if the man would allow his comments to be recorded. He did not object, and Rambar produced a small recorder provided by the captain.

As always, with electronic or mechanical equipment, Edmund had trouble getting it turned on. Shaz helped him, which was another favorable sign. Soon the informant was divulging tremendous amounts of previously unknown information. Rambar quickly realized that this was a major breakthrough and too much for him to handle on his own.

"Shaz, what are you hoping to gain by telling me all of this?" Edmund asked without showing any emotion about the treasure of intelligence being given.

"Mr. Edmund, I am very much afraid. If I have to go back, I be killed. Just want live in other country and maybe some money for me. Please, I am too afraid now. You must understand."

The man was speaking fairly decent English but not sufficiently fluent. Rambar couldn't speak either Romanian or Arabic. It was another reason to have someone with language capabilities interview him. Rambar did attempt to converse in a bit of Russian, but it was useless. Shaz shook his head, not understanding a word of it.

Taking Shaz down to the galley for something to eat and coffee, Rambar decided to contact Larry in Langley, Virginia. "This is Edmund, and I think we've struck the *mother lode* here with this guy named Shazkur. I've been talking with him for a while, but his English is limited. We need to get a translator to really grill him, in a nonthreatening way. Then he needs protection, maybe setting him up in some distant country or even a witness protection program. He's terrified of ever returning to Romania and says he'd be killed. Oh yeah, I'm recording what he tells me in case something happens to him."

"Okay, I think you're right. In fact, from what you're telling me and with what information we have on him from other sources, he's a gold mine. Keep him on board until I can set up an extraction, maybe in Crete or Naples. It's too risky to try it in Istanbul. The place is full of spies and people who'd sell their grandmother for a few lousy bucks. How does your ship's captain fit into all this, Edmund?"

"It's Captain Demetriopoulos, and he's a straight shooter. Been damned helpful about that arms-smuggling deal and now too. He's given this Shaz fellow a temporary job as a deckhand so we can keep him under wraps. He even loaned me a recorder so I can get some of the information down without writing it all."

"Good. You're on top of it like always, Edmund. I'll get a plane arranged to pick him up wherever you say and assure him that we will guarantee his safety and anonymity in some place far away from Romania," Larry stated emphatically.

"We really want this guy."

Rambar rejoined Shaz in the galley and poured coffee for himself while explaining the agency's plan to get him to a safe location and provide him a new identity, if necessary.

"We feel it would be safer for you to stay on this ship until we decide on which location to pick you up by plane. Is that agreeable with you, Shaz? You know that you're too valuable to let us risk anything bad happening."

"Okay, Edmund. I am trusting you and is much better for me to be on ship with you. Not be safe very in Romania now. Put me in good country to live, and I give you all information I have for sure."

Shaz relaxed some and slurped down more coffee with his new protector, Edmund. Later, he provided even more specific information to Edmund who recorded it all.

Three days later, the ship pulled into the harbor at Crete. This was to be the place to extract Shaz from any possible danger. Edmund would take him in a staff car, provided by the British consulate in Heraklion, to the airport. Loretta and Wanda would go along, making it appear that these were two tourist couples just seeing the sights. One can never be too careful, and a little deception often provides a lot of security, experience had taught Edmund.

Thinking of everything, Edmund had Shaz dressed like an American businessman and told him not say anything when around strangers. Waiting for them at the airport was a plane, unmarked except for its tail number, and parked at the far end of the tarmac. Outside was an operative from the CIA office in Lisbon. He greeted Shaz warmly and invited him to board.

Edmund waved goodbye to him, relieved that Shaz was safely out of his care.

Loretta had been watching Shaz board the aircraft. "Edmund, isn't that man wearing one of your new suits?" she asked.

"Yes, dear, he certainly is. He didn't have the proper clothes to wear for looking like an American. The agency bought those clothes for me anyway and will be pleased to replace them. That man is a valuable informant, and they're tickled to get their hands on him. It's a big deal, trust me, but that's all I can tell you," Edmund replied.

CHAPTER 31

Chance Meeting

The ship's company headquarters had agreed with Captain Demetriopoulos to bypass Piraeus. Due to the unexpected detour into the Black Sea, the ship was well behind schedule, and some of the cargo needed to be unloaded in other ports without further delay.

This change distressed a few of the passengers who had hoped to go into Athens for sightseeing. Wanda and Loretta were particularly disappointed. Loretta wanted to see the Parthenon while Wanda had hoped to see the ceremonial Greek soldiers wearing their ballet-looking white skirts and tight breeches.

As for Edmund, he just wanted to relax on deck. His right leg and knee had been troubling him ever since the scuffle back in Romania, and walking around much was nearly impossible. More than that, he felt as though Hunter was being neglected and wanted more attention. With his canine friend on one side and Princess on the other, he dozed contentedly on an upper deck. After encountering unusually rough Mediterranean waters, *The Pericles* docked in Naples, or Napoli, as the Italians correctly call it.

With assurances from the captain that there would be plenty of time for sightseeing in Pompeii, Wanda, Loretta, and most of the other passengers boarded buses for that ancient site. Edmund, always mindful of one reason that he was on this ship, watched cargo being unloaded and new crates brought on. Nothing unusual caught his eye as he sipped on his favorite drink.

After the long day of sightseeing, the passengers disembarked from the tour bus, filled with excitement at what they'd seen. Loretta and Wanda came back mournful after seeing body casts of the people who'd perished in both Pompeii and Herculaneum. Dinner at the captain's table was filled with conversation about what the women had seen. Rambar anticipated getting on to Nice then Monaco to show Loretta around and perhaps do a bit of gambling.

Over the night, the ship cruised over the portions of the Mediterranean known as the Tyrrhenian and Ligurian seas from Naples and into port at Nice. Fortunately, there was much cargo to unload for France. This allowed the ship to be docked until late the next day.

Leaving Hunter and Princess to frolic happily together aboard ship on a small private deck, Loretta and Edmund took off for Monte Carlo on their own.

Wanda decided to relax in one of the open-air hotel bars along the Promenade des Anglais and watch attractive-looking males.

"Why couldn't the ship dock in Monaco, Edmund? There are harbors there too, aren't there?" Loretta asked him.

"Yes, of course there are, dear. Monaco is all coastline, but the harbors are set up more for luxury yachts than freighters. Besides, from what I've noticed, most of the docks are filled up all the time," Edmund replied patiently.

"I do wish that Dorris and Nigel were still here. We'd have a great time running around together, wouldn't we?" Loretta told Edmund. "I guess by now they're back in England, huh?"

"Good thought. I'll give Nigel a call and see how they're doing," he said, reaching for his cell phone.

"Hello, Nigel, this is Edmund. Are you two safely back in the UK? You're not? What happened? Oh, that's terrible. Is Dorris all right? You're still in Monaco, eh? Well, we just arrived a short while ago." Turning toward Loretta, he explained everything to her. "Dorris slipped on some wet pavement and broke her ankle."

Then back to Nigel, "I can certainly relate to that. You probably remember that I slipped and broke my arm while here a few months back, also on wet pavement. Loretta and I would like to get together with you both, for dinner perhaps? How long are you planning on staying in Monaco?" Edmund asked.

"We would love to, old boy. Is 7:00 p.m. satisfactory to you and Loretta? Splendid. We are staying at the Hermitage and have been taking our meals in the hotel restaurant. Do you enjoy eating there too?" Nigel asked.

"Yes, you and I had lunch there with Inspector Gerard once, didn't we? Loretta will enjoy seeing that hotel, and it's so close to the casino too," Edmund mentioned.

Over dinner, they all made small talk and Loretta related what had happened to them and the dogs in Romania.

"I was so afraid that Hunter might have been badly injured and, of course, Edmund too," she said, the latter part in a joking manner.

"Ah, dear Edmund is a tough old sod and can still take care of himself," Nigel interjected. "Besides, we tend to worry more about our animals than we do about ourselves, don't we? This is right too because it's rather difficult to find a good dog. You can always find some old gaffer who'll do well enough," Nigel replied jokingly.

"Hm, thank you so much, both of you," Edmund retorted. "I guess that I know where I stand now," he affected a *hurt* look at them.

Turning more serious, he asked Nigel if he was aware of a recent weapon being developed by several countries. "This is the hypersonic missile called the ARRP, an acronym for Air-Launched Rapid Response Projectile."

"I've only just been reading about it, Edmund. Don't really know much yet. But I'm sure that as new weapons are developed, there will be many governments interested in getting their hands on any information they can."

"This will probably go on forever until we finally manage to destroy ourselves and the planet. It's sad, really, and I'm getting too old to keep up with it all. I've been so technologically challenged anyway...," Edmund mused, his voice trailing off.

"We will be going home when we leave this splendid little country," Dorris told everyone. "Nigel really must return to work, and I should get back to my charitable efforts. Are you two staying with the ship back to the States or visiting other parts of Europe on your own?"

"We really haven't talked about it. What do you think, Edmund?" Loretta asked him.

"Whatever you'd like to see, dear heart. If you'd enjoy spending a few days in say, Paris or London, we sure can while we're here anyway. I do have one thought myself. A day or two in Gibraltar could be interesting. I've never been there, just looked at it from the ship. How do you feel about it, Loretta?"

"It could be kind of fun as long as I'm with you, Edmund. Don't they have some kind of monkeys living up on the rock there?" she asked, turning toward Nigel.

"Yes. As you know, Gibraltar is one of ours and a strategic naval base as well. Those animals are barbary apes, and while they remain there, Britain will always control that colony. It's something like the ravens at the Tower of London," Nigel informed them.

"I believe that I could arrange a tour for you to see the inner workings of our operations here. In fact, it's been ages since I last visited that colony, and it could be worthwhile for me to pop in there myself. You know, something like *showing the flag* and all that. We don't want any of our territories to think that we've forgotten about them or that they're not a vital part of the empire. Provided Dorris doesn't mind extending our holiday a bit longer, we could continue on to Lisbon and then drive over to Gib for a day or two. How do you feel about it, Edmund?"

"That would be great, Nigel. We both love your company, and the longer we keep it, the better. Is it okay with you, Loretta?"

"Well, I don't mind seeing it with you, Edmund, but perhaps Dorris and I could just skip Lisbon and fly up to Paris from Barcelona instead. I know you've been there before and could show me around. Would you enjoy doing it that way, Dorris?

"I think that would be a splendid idea, Loretta. After all, we have already visited both Barcelona and Lisbon on our way east. While Gibraltar could be worth seeing, I'd rather show you around Paris, and we could do some shopping. I'd be delighted to act as your tour guide, and my ankle is much better now," Dorris said, smiling back.

"It would give us more time for 'girl talk' too, away from our men and so on," Loretta answered, quite pleased at the prospect.

"Of course, if that's what you two would enjoy, then by all means, let's do it that way," Edmund said, confirming the decision. He exchanged a knowing glance at Nigel, both of them realizing it would easier not having the women along while they did some classified work.

It was decided that Hunter would remain with Edmund. When the ship docked in Lisbon, Wanda would watch both dogs as they played together on board. After driving to Gibraltar and conferring with the officials there, the men would return and wait until Loretta flew back to Lisbon. Dorris was somewhat anxious about returning to London and decided to go back home right after Paris.

Because they would gain some time while the ship unloaded cargo at both ports, in Spain and then Portugal, Edmund and Loretta could reboard it again in Lisbon. Then after a brief stopover in the Canary Islands, they'd sail back to the States, completing their ocean voyage vacation. Captain Demetriopoulos assured them that it would be awaiting them at the dock in the Portuguese capital.

CHAPTER 32

At Gibraltar

With the women safely aboard their flight to Paris, the men could talk freely about classified matters.

"Edmund, I *actually am* somewhat familiar with the ARRP missile program. I know they do have the capability of speeds up to twenty times that of conventional weapons. Didn't want to divulge too much in front of our lovely companions. Most secret stuff, as you know.

"The UK is a relatively small place, and we do not intend to put all of our weaponry in one basket, as you might say. We still have a few strategic colonies, but unfortunately, like Gibraltar, they tend to be of extremely limited land area. One could hardly place much tactical ordinance onto say, Pitcairn or Saint Helena.

"Much of our nuclear arsenal is at various highly classified locations within the Commonwealth. This brings us back to the ARRP missiles. Both the UK and the US have been jointly developing them for some time now, and we will soon have working models. Again, I am compelled to ask your assistance in conveying some classified information over to your government.

"You can again utilize the ring you used previously. It will now be waiting for us at Gib since you decided to stop there. Otherwise, it would be in London. Not sure just how that could have worked out. You would have need to modify your itinerary, perhaps a bit tricky with Hunter along."

"Yes, of course, I'll do it, Nigel. How could I refuse having come this far? We do make a good team, don't we?"

"Indeed, we do, old boy, and I'll miss working with you now that we've become such good friends. Ah well, I shall soon be retired myself. Hopefully Her Majesty's government will let me stay retired better than yours has done with you," Nigel replied somewhat seriously.

Being well up the northeastern coast of Spain, the return trip took nearly three full days. They backtracked their same route: south, then west, through the Strait of Gibraltar to Lisbon. Once docked, Edmund and Nigel rented a small car and drove across into Spain.

At Algeciras, they crossed into Gibraltar. After a short delay waiting for a plane to land at the airport, they proceeded. The small runway intersected the highway between Spain and the colony, always causing traffic problems when the crossing gates went down.

By now, it was late afternoon, and they decided to rent a hotel room before going over to Royal Navy (RN) headquarters the next day. With only a few hotels available, it was impossible to avoid hearing the raucous brawling of drunken British tourists on the main street. For some reason, the colony attracted newly affluent lower-class types who could afford the price of a few sunny days outside the UK. These people skipped most historic sites and the barbary apes, devoting themselves to drinking and fighting each other.

After a less then restful night and a dinner of overcooked food, the men freshened up and proceeded over to the RN offices. Identifying themselves, they were warmly welcomed by the naval commander Admiral Tollerton. He escorted them first to the officers' dining room for tea and scones, which they gratefully devoured.

"I'm afraid that the dining here in town is woefully lacking in both quality and preparation. Would you gentlemen enjoy something a bit more substantial than the scones? Our chef would be quite pleased to cook you a proper English breakfast if you feel slightly peckish."

Without waiting for agreement by Edmund, Nigel immediately took advantage of the offer. "Yes, definitely. After the wretched meal we suffered through last night, anything at all would be much appreciated."

Edmund offered his comments. "Even kippers spread with marmite would be gratefully accepted though I don't much care for either of 'em. Thank you so much for considering our plight for something edible."

They enjoyed a good chuckle about the food situation, then got down to business. While being given a VIP tour of the operations center deep inside the Rock, Nigel asked if the commander had been briefed by London about the well-traveled ring that Edmund would wear.

"Yes, we have it ready for you, filled with the intelligence to be carried. Our experience has been that this is much more secure than using electronic means with codes. Your reputation has proceeded you, Mr. Rambar. Having heard of your previous missions of this type, we are most pleased you are willing to do this. A discreet escort will be close by until you are safely back in Washington, DC. Much the same procedure as on your other courier trips. Both for your own safety and that of the information you'll carry, we couldn't have you running loose on your own without backup. Of course, you know all that," Tollerton said.

"The Israelis are interested in the ARRP program as well. They are our friends, but we can't just go sharing with every country who might want it. They have been damned clever about getting what they want, and I'll have to give *that* to them. Persistent little devils. They *must be*, considering where they are and who surrounds their territory. However, mugging somebody for information isn't their style, Edmund, so you can feel secure in that regard, as you know," Admiral Tollerton went on.

"Anyway, enough about that for now. I have a young agent whom I'd like to introduce. His name is Kirk Hanrahan. In fact, Nigel, I dare say you may know him. He's new with MI6 and has excellent skills and credentials. We were glad he came on board here in Gibraltar. Let me get him down here so he can meet Mr. Rambar."

Waiting for Hanrahan to arrive, Admiral Tollerton told them a bit more about the man. "He's twenty-seven or twenty-eight years of age and a martial arts master. Came from Northern Ireland, I think. He's also fluent in two or three foreign languages as well. A delightful young fellow and quite deadly, if need be."

"Yes, I have met him, Admiral. He is new with our office and most highly recommended," Nigel recalled. "I'm thinking that he will accompany Edmund for the remainder of his trip back to the States?"

"Quite. Ah, here he is now. Kirk, I believe you know Nigel Brown, don't you? This is Mr. Edmund Rambar, and we would like you to accompany him while he transports some intelligence to Washington. It will be mostly by ship, and likely a pleasant trip for you," the Admiral explained.

With the introductions over, it was decided that Rambar and Hanrahan would not know each other until *accidentally* meeting aboard ship. However, they would return to Lisbon by helicopter provided by the admiral rather than drive back through Spain into Portugal. It's a safer and quicker alternative than going by car.

"Let's get you fitted with your special ring, Rambar, and I'll brief Kirk while doing that."

"What about the car Nigel and I rented in Lisbon? We'll need to return it somewhere," Edmund mentioned.

"Don't feel concerned about that. We'll have one of our people drive it over to Algeciras and turn it in," Tollerton assured him.

Later, Edmund and Kirk took Nigel over to the small airport for a GB Airways flight to London and home.

"A pity you and Loretta couldn't spend some time with us in the UK but perhaps next time. Or with a bit of luck, we will get over to Wyoming and visit you," Nigel effused sincerely.

CHAPTER 33

Talking Shop with Kirk

As their chopper flew westbound, Rambar got acquainted with Kirk Hanrahan.

God, I'm nearly old enough to be his great-grandfather, he thought, feeling his soon-to-be eighty years, tired and with his knee throbbing. *What the heck's his first name anyway? It is definitely a bitch to get old.*

"Perhaps it could be more advisable for me to be booking passage on your ship before you return to it. Would you be thinking that way yourself, sir?" Kirk asked politely, with a noticeable Gaelic brogue. "I'm going to be an Irish folk singer myself, leaving a gig in Lisbon and en route to the States for a while as my *cover* story."

"Good, Kirk," he said, remembering his name. "I kind of wondered why you brought along a guitar," Edmund replied. "Shouldn't be any problem for you to get on board. If you plan to do some entertaining as part of your passage, that would be an excellent *cover*. I'm sure the captain will agree because there's nothing except recorded music available. Please call me Edmund, not *sir*. I feel ancient enough as it is. You're from Northern Ireland. Is that right?"

Young Hanrahan smiled appreciatively and felt more relaxed as they continued talking. "I'm really from the Republic, born near Dublin. I have dual citizenship and carry both Irish and UK passports. Fortunately, MI6 felt that I'd be a good risk anyway," he joked. "With total respect, sir, that is, Edmund, are you not perhaps a bit old to be doing this game yet? Which, to be sure, makes me wonder why you're doing it?"

"I'm not really too sure about that myself, but I suppose it's a number of different reasons. About seventeen years ago, I retired from the agency and, at the time, was happy doing so. But my son and his wife needed some help buying a house, and I loaned them quite a lot of money.

"When a former partner of mine and a good friend came to my place and offered me some sizeable CIA cash for a onetime courier run, I took it. To be completely honest, I kind of missed the work, and it was supposed to be a simple thing. Like everything that looks easy on the surface, it turned into a more complex, even dangerous operation. By then, I was so involved that I had to see it through," Edmund continued.

"Well, I finally made it home and thought that would be *it*. Not so. My fiancée and I decided to take a Mediterranean cruise. The agency called and asked me to just keep my eyes open for any activity that might interest the agency. That's what I've been doing.

"By a sheer coincidence, we happened to meet up with Nigel and his wife on the same cruise. It was wonderful to encounter them because I knew him from my previous mission in London. Turns out he was doing about the same thing I was—looking for any illegal goings-on that would interest MI6. Naturally we found some, which started another adventure. I won't go into that right now.

"Anyway, I'd mentioned that it would interest me to see Gibraltar. Nigel offered to introduce me to the naval operations people there, which he did. I got the grand tour and then the admiral in charge asked me to take some intelligence back to my agency in the States. I could hardly refuse, which is where you came in, Kirk."

"So then, one thing just led to another, and you're doing courier duty again. You are indeed a remarkable man, Edmund. It's an honor to be working with you, and I have no doubt that I'll be learning many things while we're traveling together."

By now, the chopper reached Lisbon airport, and they parted company for the moment. Kirk headed for the dock to *The Pericles*. Rambar entered the terminal building, and almost immediately, he heard the welcoming voice of Loretta.

"I'm over here, Edmund, and I'm so glad you came to get me. I wasn't sure if I should just take a taxi to the ship or when you might be here. This has worked out perfectly, dear. Dorris was a great tour guide, and she knows that city so well, every nook and cranny. We've become such good friends, and we must have them over to Wyoming very soon."

"I wondered when your plane would arrive. Just got here now, myself. Took a helicopter over from Gibraltar instead of driving back. Nigel flew home from there. Gibraltar was fascinating, but I think you enjoyed Paris more than you might have there."

"Shall we take a taxi back to the ship now, or are you hungry, Edmund?"

"Let's eat on board. I'd like to have a drink with Captain Demetriopoulos, and we can have a better dinner there. I hate most airport food, don't you, dear heart?"

Meanwhile, Kirk had arrived at the ship and was speaking with the first officer about getting a ticket. He mentioned that he was coming off a gig in Portugal and offered to put on a one-man show for the passengers. After looking at the young man's crisp new Irish passport and conferring briefly with the captain, it was arranged. A crewman showed him to a cabin next to Rambar and Loretta's.

A short while later they arrived, Edmund was carrying a large bag full of things Loretta had bought in Paris. He had hoped to lie down for a while but was hungry enough to forgo a nap. They headed for the dining room just as dinner was being served. Wanda was there with both dogs, planning to feed them table scraps.

"Oh, Loretta, I'm so glad you're back. Did you have a good time? The dogs missed you greatly. You can see how happy they are to see you again," she said as both dogs wagged their tails excitedly.

The door opened into the dining room, and Kirk entered, smiling. "It must surely be dinner now, and I'm smelling most inviting," he said ingratiatingly.

The captain stood to announce him. "Ladies and gentlemen, we are in for a big treat this evening. It is my pleasure to have you meet Kirk Hanrahan who will entertain everyone with his Irish folk songs and guitar."

There was a round of applause and Kirk blushed slightly. "You have already met our second new passenger, Mr. Zoltan Marzinzsc, who joined us earlier. Did I pronounce your name correctly, sir?"

The dark-complexed man, seated at another table, bowed slightly but said nothing. Kirk found a place at the table directly across from Wanda, who smiled invitingly. Her cougar radar went up immediately. She *liked*. He smiled back pleasantly not picking up her signal.

After dinner, Rambar joined the captain for a drink at the bar. He decided to not inform him about Kirk's real reason for being on the ship. Describing his visit to Gibraltar, he omitted anything about meeting with officials there, only mentioning the usual tourist attractions. Now he wanted to get back to his and Loretta's cabin and rest.

* * *

At CIA headquarters in Langley, Edmund's friend Larry has been briefed that Rambar would be carrying intelligence when arriving at Biloxi in a few days.

In the Eastern US, the time was about 2:30 p.m., so Rambar decided to call Larry about arranging the promised flight back home.

"I hear you're wearing some expensive *jewelry* again, Edmund. You have something for your friends here, right?" Larry opened the conversation.

"Yes, Larry, I found a nice ring that you'll find interesting. When we reach Biloxi, who should I give it to?"

"The plan is that I'll wander on down there myself and get it from you. Yes, you will definitely have a plane there ready to take you, Loretta, and pooch back home. No sweat because you're a VIP in our eyes, you old coot."

CHAPTER 34

Encounter with Borenko

During the two-day cruise over to the Canary Islands, Kirk and Rambar spent much time talking shop while the two ladies, Loretta and Wanda, walked the dogs around for exercise.

"Kirk, I'm really out of date with all of this new tech knowledge and the electronic assets now available. Terms that are now commonplace completely mystify me, which is why my low-tech approach is an asset in itself. I have no idea what quantum entanglement, parallel universes, or synthetic DNA might be. I'm just an old man who has no desire to learn anything new at this point. My eightieth birthday is coming up soon, and I want to be doing things that I want to do and enjoy my time with Loretta and Hunter."

"I do believe that I'm understanding you, Edmund. Life is short enough to not make it as pleasant as we are able. As I've heard said by some Americans, 'Life sucks, then you die.' Sure, now you want to being getting on with your retirement plans, without a doubt. So I'll be trying to help you however I can."

"You're a fine young man, Kirk, and I'd be most honored to have you as my grandson. I'm glad we're on this assignment together," Edmund replied, grasping his hand warmly.

* * *

Arriving at Santa Cruz on Tenerife island in the Canary, Loretta and Wanda were eager to go ashore and explore the place and, of course, shop. Edmund wanted to talk more with Kirk on board but agreed to meet them for dinner and drinks later. While the Spanish prefer to enjoy their dinner well into the night, often around 10:00 or 11:00 p.m., most North Americans and Northern Europeans can't wait.

At six in the evening, Loretta called Edmund and told him, "We found a *perfectly darling little café* to eat at."

Edmund agreed and told them that Kirk would be joining them. Wanda, the cougar, was excited, looking forward with anticipation. Loretta liked young Kirk too, but more as an indulgent aunt. When the men arrived, she couldn't wait to tell Edmund about the interesting man they'd met earlier while having coffee.

"Oh, he's just the most fascinating man, Edmund. I'm sure you'd enjoy meeting him. He's probably a bit younger than you, and he's been all over the world. I think he's with a trade delegation or something. He's from, was it Ruthenia or Russia? Well, I'm not sure, but he speaks English fairly well and is very charming."

Just politely listening, her chattering was of only slight interest to Edmund. "Did you happen to get his name or where we could perhaps meet him?"

"Oh, what did he say his name was, Wanda, do you remember?"

Wanda thought for a moment, concentrating more on Kirk than the conversation. "Yes, I'm pretty sure he said it was Victor."

Edmund's ears pricked up immediately. The image of his enemy, Borenko, popped into his conscious. Kirk began listening carefully too. They had talked about the narrow escapes by Rambar from the Russian's murder attempts.

"Can you describe him, Loretta? It's just possible that I know who he is. Tell me anything you remember about him," Edmund pursued gently.

"Well, he had a bad limp and was probably very arthritic. His hands were quite stiff, and his knuckles seemed swollen. But he was such a nice man that I didn't notice too much about his appearance," Loretta continued, unaware of Edmund's growing concern. "Oh, yes, I seem to remember that his last name began with a *B*, something like Boroko, I think."

"Did you happen to give him your name or mine, dear heart?" Edmund persevered.

"No, I'm sure I didn't because just after he introduced himself, another man he was with said he was wanted on the cell phone. We were eager to get back to a little shop we'd found, and so we left," Loretta explained.

"I'll tell you more later, dear love, but for now we have to be very careful if we should run into him while we're here," he cautioned her.

"What happened? Were you enemies when you were working, Edmund?"

"Yes, something like that. He's a Russian agent, and he tried to kill me. Would have done it too, if he could. He thinks that he was successful and doesn't know that I'm alive. It's best to avoid him while we're here. I don't want to endanger you or Wanda. He and his friends tried to harm Hunter too."

"Oh no, Edmund. Should we just go back to the ship?" she asked, very disturbed.

"No, I don't think so. We're inside and let's enjoy a nice dinner. I didn't mean to worry you ladies," he replied, trying to sound confident.

People were beginning to come into the restaurant, among them were two Russians, one of whom was Borenko. He didn't notice the women seated at a far table with Kirk and Edmund. After eating more quickly than normal, they got up to leave.

Closer to the door, Borenko looked up, not sure if he actually saw what he thought he had, as they passed.

Looking out the window, he realized that it *was* Rambar, still very much alive. He said something to his companion in a low voice, and they got up to leave.

"Why did he not die from bomb I put in car for him?" Borenko fumed. "This time he not escape, that bastard," speaking excitedly in Russian.

With the ladies in their cabins, Kirk and Edmund walked Hunter around the deck while discussing the situation. It was twilight, not yet sufficiently dark enough to turn on the outside lighting. By now, it was turning cool, and Kirk offered to retrieve Edmund's jacket that he'd left inside. Toward the bow of the ship, Zoltan Marzinzsc was standing unnoticed, having a smoke.

The gangway was still down awaiting the return of other passengers who had gone ashore. Two men in seaman's clothing walked up onto the vessel, then went in different directions along the deck. One of them limped badly as he walked closer toward Rambar.

Hunter woofed when he saw the second man approaching from the starboard side. Edmund turned to see him. From the back, now almost upon him, the first man held a commando-type knife.

"Edvard, this is last day for you. Now you die," Borenko told him *soto voce*. He stabbed forcefully as Rambar tried to deflect the blade with his right arm. The second Russian approached and tried to grab Edmund. Hunter powerfully lunged at the man. His fangs bit into the neck of the assailant who recoiled, wounded.

Borenko's knife cut into Rambar's shirt sleeve but struck only his watchband.

Kirk had just returned to the deck. Ever alert, he ran to the fray and threw the jacket over Borenko, pulling him away from Edmund. In a swift, skillful motion, he twisted the Russian's head, snapping his neck. He was dead when he fell to the deck.

At the same moment, the mysterious Zoltan Marzinzsc grabbed the other Russian from behind, who was still retreating from the snarling dog. In the same manner as Kirk's, he silently dispatched the man, who dropped down, lifeless.

Unhurt, Edmund reached down and petted Hunter, praising him gratefully. He then turned to thank Zoltan, who announced, "I am an agent with MI6 as you are too, Kirk. Like yourself, I've been assigned to protect Mr. Rambar."

"That makes sense, Zoltan. You didn't look much like a tourist when the captain introduced us. I had thought you could surely be a foreign operative, but indeed, no one knew Mr. Rambar was carrying intelligence information except for Nigel and myself. In any case, we are extremely glad to be seeing yourself."

"Quite true, Kirk. Now, gentlemen, we must dispose of these two bodies before anyone sees what we've been doing," Zoltan said urgently. "If we can get them off the ship and down on the dock unnoticed, I think we'll be *in the clear*, as the Americans say."

With some difficulty, they got the bodies upright and staggered them down the gangway, acting as if they were helping their drunken pals. No one was in sight as they dropped them behind some large crates way down the dock.

Back on the ship, Kirk hurried down to his cabin, retrieving his guitar. After all, he had a show to do for the passengers in the dining salon. When he took the stage, he apologized. "I am so very, very regretful for being late, but I had something to *drop off* in town." Then he launched into a version of "Whiskey in the Jar" to everyone's delight.

"Isn't he wonderful?" Wanda exclaimed, delighted.

"Yes, even more so than you can imagine, Wanda," Edmund replied, winking at Zoltan.

Shortly after the evening meal, the ship departed westbound for the Atlantic crossing. There were to be no additional stops until the port of Biloxi. Edmund ordered drinks for everyone in the dining salon, and he toasted both Kirk and Zoltan though no one knew exactly why.

CHAPTER 35

Engine Problems

After dinner, the three men went on deck for a smoke. When they were alone, away from any other passengers, Zoltan pulled out some things from his coat pocket. These were two Russian diplomatic passports, two wallets, and various other papers, anything which could identify the two men they killed.

He handed the passports over to Rambar for burial at sea.

"Goodbye, Borenko, you lose," Edmund said while ripping the documents apart and tossing them into the Atlantic. Then Zoltan let both wallets fall into the water, and Kirk tore up the other papers and did the same.

"They should have left you alone, and they'd still be among the living," Kirk commented dryly. "I doubt if the Russian government will ever acknowledge their deaths even if they will find out what happened. More likely there will be an announcement on Radio Moscow that Borenko retired to his dacha east of the capital. Nothing will probably ever be said about the second man. The records will just show him as missing."

The fact that both deceased men were wearing seaman's clothes would further delay the Spanish police from making an identification of them. Initially it would be assumed that two drunken merchant sailors had been mugged, then killed by thieves.

While there is some fingerprinting identification in use worldwide, it is far from universally exchanged. It's doubtful that the Russians participate in submitting fingerprints of their citizens to an international crime-solving pool. Therefore, it could be difficult to ever identify the two men's bodies left on the dock at the Canary Island of Tenerife.

* * *

The next few days went by peacefully with most of the travelers eager to get back home and tell everyone about their adventures. Loretta, Edmund, and Wanda lounged on the deck in canvas chairs, sipping cool drinks. The two dogs were with them, sprawled out in the afternoon sun. Everyone was relaxed and content.

"Do you think that Russian man would have still been mad enough to want to harm you, Edmund?" Loretta asked.

"I really couldn't say. Maybe he just decided it wasn't worth trying it again. I have a strong feeling that we won't see him again."

* * *

Late one afternoon, the sky suddenly darkened. It ominously warned of another frequent Atlantic storm soon to be upon the ship. It grew much cooler, and everyone on deck decided to go inside.

Wanda's dog, Princess, had gotten loose and raced around on the deck, her leash trailing behind. The wind and lightning flashes frightened her, and she yelped excitedly. Kirk grabbed her, petting and speaking soothingly as he carried her into the salon. Grateful, Wanda hugged Kirk and kissed him on the cheek.

"I have a bottle of good Irish whiskey in my cabin. Could I offer you a drink, Kirk?" she asked invitingly.

"Well, sure now, I've never been known to turn down a dram of the pure," he replied. "But maybe just one for now or perhaps two— to calm our nerves with the storm and all."

"Would you like to take Princess to your cabin so she and Hunter can be together?" Wanda asked Loretta.

"Oh sure, I think they'd both feel more secure until this storm is over," Loretta replied, taking the poodle's leash.

Wanda, with Kirk in tow, retreated to her cabin as she smiled wickedly to herself. She had made it her goal to *have* him before the voyage was over. Inside, she poured them stiff drinks and offered a toast to "new friends and a delightful trip."

They started on a third drink, with Wanda's much smaller than Kirk's. He felt slightly drowsy, sipping slower on the whiskey, as Wanda watched him intently. The storm raged on more fiercely than before. This was an older ship and not equipped with gyrostabilizers, so it rocked around annoyingly. Still, Kirk was fully relaxed, and the motion made him feel cradled, not uncomfortable.

At one sudden lurch, Wanda *accidentally* fell right onto Kirk who was sitting on the edge of her bed. In an apparent attempt to get up, she put her left arm around his shoulders.

"Now I want you to be completely honest with me, Wanda. I'm pretty certain you've had your eyes on me ever since I was coming aboard, haven't you now?" Kirk asked her teasingly.

"Yes, I have, you handsome man. I've wanted to be with you like this, desperately. Could you perhaps feel the same about me, or am I too old for your taste?" she asked seriously.

"I'm preferring more mature women anyway. A good chum of mine once told me this: 'They don't yell. They don't swell, and they're grateful as hell,' and that's my feeling too."

He pulled her down on top of him and kissed her deeply as they breathed heavily with whiskey-scented breaths. She slid her right hand down onto the obvious bulge at his crotch and stroked him gently. He undid her blouse and felt her taut breasts. She was wearing no bra and felt warm to his touch. He put down his head and nibbled and tongued them affectionately.

The ship lurched heavily as they rolled around on the bed.

"Maybe I should tie you up, Kirk, so you won't fall out of my bed," Wanda teased, partly serious.

"I don't think I could let you be doing that now although I might perhaps be liking it. If this ship was sinking, how could I be saving you with my hands all tied?" Kirk joked back.

Wanda skillfully unhooked his belt and pulled down the zipper of his pants. She'd had considerable practice in doing it, then she felt the stretched fabric of his tight black briefs. Being orally inclined, she went down slowly as he tensed every muscle.

* * *

There was a sudden audible banging sound heard throughout the entire ship. It kept repeating steadily. Back in their own cabin, Edmund decided to go up to the captain's wheel room. "I'll find out what's going on," he told Loretta and petted both dogs reassuringly.

Arriving, he found Captain Demetriopoulos fervently checking gauges and speaking with the crewmen down in the engine room. Edmund waited patiently until the captain turned toward him.

"It appears that we are having some engine problems. It sounds like a bad cylinder, but I'm having the engine room men investigate it right now," he told Rambar. "I will inform the passengers as soon as we determine the problem."

In a few minutes, the defective engine was shut down while the others pushed the vessel forward at a very reduced speed. The frightening noise ceased.

Everyone in their cabins waited apprehensively for an announcement from the bridge.

"Everyone, do not be concerned. We are having some engine problems, but there is no danger whatsoever. We are quite close to Bermuda, and I have ordered that our ship will dock there to assess the problem and make repairs," the captain reassured the passengers and crew.

Approximately sixty nautical miles distant, it would take four hours to reach the Crown Colony. The storm was abating much to everyone's relief. It would be much smoother now. Several passengers had migrated to the dining salon and were discussing their situation.

Loretta had joined Edmund there. Always the optimist, she cheerfully told him, "Oh good. We get to see another place before getting back to the States."

* * *

Being a young vital man, Kirk had quickly *recharged* and was powerfully emmeshed with Wanda, who clawed at him hungrily. Their passion built for another round as they stopped to have still more whiskey.

"I wonder what that banging noise was?" Wanda asked Kirk.

"Well, I'm thinking surely it wasn't us although it could well have been with all the carrying on we were doing," he replied, still breathing heavily.

"Maybe we should be taking a break now, and I'll find out what it was. Reluctant though it is for me to be leaving you, even for a minute."

Quickly pulling his clothes on, he ran up to the deck and encountered Zoltan.

"Didn't you hear the captain's announcement in your cabin, Kirk?"

"No, I must have been sleeping or something," he lied. "I didn't hear a thing except for whatever that banging sound happened to be. Would you be knowing anything about it, Zoltan?"

"The captain said it was some kind of problem with the engine, so we're going to stop in Bermuda. I think it's about four or five hours away. He said there's no danger, just a broken cylinder or whatever."

* * *

Rambar, fully aware that the information he was carrying in his ring was highly important, decided to call Larry at CIA headquarters. Reaching him by phone, Larry reiterated the urgency of it. He decided to fly out to Bermuda and take the ring instead of waiting for the ship to reach Biloxi. It was uncertain just how long the repairs could take before they could continue on.

Rambar concurred, somewhat eager to relinquish the intelligence contained in the ring. It would be a relief to him and Kirk and Zoltan. He met with them shortly and explained his conversation with Larry. This changed the situation considerably. Zoltan now planned to return to London once they arrived in Bermuda. Kirk, wanting more action with Wanda, contacted MI6 and decided to take a few more days aboard, with their approval.

On hearing this, Wanda was delighted. She and Kirk resumed rutting like wild boars in season. Edmund told Loretta that he had spoken with Larry and that he would be meeting them in Hamilton at the airport. They could see the sights while the ship was being repaired, a happy prospect that pleased Loretta greatly.

CHAPTER 36

Rambar Sees Helen

While walking along Front Street in downtown Hamilton, looking in the shop windows, they were deciding where to have lunch. Hunter was with them and was enjoying his outing off the ship. Wanda remined onboard with Kirk, but Zoltan followed discreetly, possibly with others behind him.

Then they heard someone call out, "Is that you, Lord Rancourt?"

Edmund looked around and saw a young woman heading toward them. She looked familiar, and then he recognized her. It was Helen, one of his shadows in London. "My goodness, Helen, what are you doing here in Bermuda?"

Again, she addressed him as Lord Rancourt, which confused Loretta.

"Is that woman mistaking you for someone else, Edmund?" Loretta asked him.

"Um, this is a bit embarrassing, ladies. I owe you both an explanation. Helen, this is my fiancée, Loretta. We were on a cruise in the Mediterranean and are now en route back to the States. Our ship developed engine problems and we pulled in here for repairs."

"You don't sound British now, Lord Rancourt," Helen seemed confused. "I don't understand, but you do have a good American accent."

"It's time for me to come clean about all this. Could we have lunch? And I'll explain everything," Edmund assured them both.

Over plates of wonderful tasting seafood, he began. "First, Loretta, this is one of the dear people who helped protect me while I was in London last year. I was on a courier assignment for my old agency, the CIA. As you know, I retired some years ago, but they offered me a huge incentive to take on one last mission to London. So I did.

"In deep cover as a British nobleman, I was able to throw off any suspicion as to what I was really doing. It worked quite successfully too. When my part in it was completed, I planned to return to the States and to you, dear Loretta.

"The UK government offered to send me down to the French Riviera on a paid holiday if I would just take something to the police in Monaco. I was quite tired from all the excitement in London, so I accepted their offer. I flew into Nice then by bus to Monaco. Helen and her new partner Jack accompanied me. Then since I needed to return to London for my flight home, I agreed to carry some information back to MI6.

"You see, Helen, I am really an American. However, there was a mole in our organization in the States. He told his UK counterparts to be looking for an elderly American man with a limp. Thus, the charade as Lord Rancourt. As you know, Loretta. I finally got back home. Thinking that my operational days with the agency were over, I wanted to take you on a nice, quiet vacation somewhere. We decided on a cruise, and here we are. That's an abbreviated version."

"What brings you to Bermuda, Helen? Are you on an assignment or something?" Edmund asked, turning back to her.

"Actually, I'm on holiday with my boyfriend, Alec. At the moment, he's out fishing and wanted me to try it with him. But Hamilton is such an interesting town that I thought I'd stay and look around. Fortunate that I did, isn't it?"

"Yes, what a remarkable coincidence this is. Oh, and speaking of coincidences, Loretta and I happened to be on the same cruise ship as Nigel Brown and his wife, Dorris," Edmund continued.

"Quite extraordinary, really. Still, these things just sort of happen sometimes," Helen said, pleasantly surprised. "I do see Nigel quite often on the job, so to speak."

"We've met some other delightful people too," Loretta added. "You might remember a movie star from a while back named Wanda Wendover. She's on this cruise too, along with her dog. We have our dog too. His name is Hunter. Unfortunately, we've met some horrible people too. Edmund almost got his wallet stolen in a shopping area of Istanbul. Then we were just walking along a dock in some Romanian town when a strange man kicked Wanda's dog, Princess. Hunter ran to her rescue but the man began beating him until we stopped it. Oh, just terrible. I don't want to even talk about it," Loretta said, almost in tears.

"Then in the Canary Islands, we nearly encountered a Russian agent who was still mad at Edmund for some reason. Luckily, we avoided him and made it back to our ship before he could do anything."

"By any chance, was his name Viktor Borenko?" Helen asked with sudden interest.

"Why, yes. How did you know that, Helen?" Loretta responded in amazement.

"He was someone we crossed swords with a few times. A very dangerous man. I'm glad you didn't have to deal with him," Helen said with relief.

Edmund winked at her. "I'll have to tell you about it sometime soon, Helen."

Excusing herself, Loretta headed for the ladies' room. Alone with Edmund, Helen urged him to explain what had happened with Borenko.

"I didn't want to frighten Loretta, but he followed us later to the ship and came aboard with a friend of his. Seeing me alone on the deck, they jumped on me, intending murder. Viktor lunged at me with a knife, cutting my shirt sleeve. Fortunately, he struck my watchband instead of my arm. Just then, my new shadow Kirk came back on deck, ran up, and dispatched him, permanently.

"The second Russian came at me from behind. I didn't even see him. A young man, standing in the shadows farther down the deck, saw him. Bounding quickly to my assistance, he grabbed him and snapped his neck. Turns out that young fellow is with your agency too. His name is Zoltan and was an assigned as a second backup for me. Please tell Nigel about Borenko. He'll be interested."

Loretta returned just as Helen was departing. "I had best be going now. Alec will be getting back from his fishing expedition."

As Helen left, Loretta told Edmund, "I think there's an awful lot of things that I don't know about you, Edmund. And the more I learn, it makes me love and respect you even more," she told him sincerely.

He looked at her with great affection. "I feel the same about you, dear love. We probably care for each other nearly as much as we do for Hunter," he said. She understood and kissed him on the top of his head.

"Now we must get to the airport and meet Larry."

* * *

Out at Bermuda's only airport, the L. F. Wade International, Loretta and Edmund watched the Boeing 737 land smoothly. Larry was one of the first passengers to deplane, and he smiled when he saw them.

"Do you have time to look around Hamilton with us and have dinner later on?" Edmund asked, hoping for some time to talk with him.

"Gee, I'd really like to, folks, but I'm going back on the next plane. I've been here before, so it's not that I'd be seeing something new. Still, I do wish I could spend more time with you both…but," Larry told them and looked genuinely disappointed.

Edmund quietly slipped the ring off his finger. Although it was on tight and difficult to do, it eventually came free. Larry took it and carefully placed it in a pouch inside his shirt. There were two men nearby who observed the transfer.

"Those guys are my escorts until I get the ring back to Langley," Larry explained. "You two enjoy the rest of your cruise. Bye-bye for now. Don't do anything I wouldn't do."

"Oh, by the way, Borenko is dead. Do you want details?" Edmund offered.

"Not really, just glad he's no longer a problem," Larry said nonchalantly.

CHAPTER 37

Houses Burglarized

Back in Wyoming, a stranger to the area had opened a new business in the small city of Casper. He called it *The New Frontier Mortuary Service*. The man had come into town, rented a small building, and stocked it with a few coffins. After having it decorated in a dignified funereal manner, he opened for clients.

Describing him accurately would be difficult because of a strange feeling that he left people with after meeting him. Physically, he was middle-aged, thin build, with graying hair, and had a noticeable overbite. Always well dressed and groomed, he spoke softly and articulately. Still, there was something unsettling about his manner and his expressionless face.

In short, the man was a con artist, using his funeral home as a *front* for other activities. He was also a thief, an opportunistic burglar, and given to fiendishly clever comments and double entendre. This latter attribute was proven by the fake name he chose, Obadiah Sepulcher. However, his business card read, Obadiah S. E. Pulcher. Such was his perverse sense of humor.

The old geezers down at the diner in Rambar's town decided that the new funeral home in the next town over was a fitting subject for conversation. One member of their group named Ernie had died recently, and his family decided to use this new mortuary.

Mr. Pulcher had made arrangements with a larger outfit in Casper to do the embalming and other prep work. This being a fairly common thing among smaller mortuaries. Digging of the graves was done by young people looking for work for which he paid them less than minimum wage. The urns and caskets were manufactured by a company in the south that made *knockoffs* of quality products. He did nothing himself except charge exorbitant fees to the bereaved families.

Meanwhile in Bermuda, it became apparent that the ship couldn't be fully repaired there. Needing more extensive work, the captain, after conferring with his corporate headquarters, decided to nurse it over to the port at Miami. Dutifully he informed the remaining passengers of the situation. Some decided to fly home from Bermuda while the rest would continue on and leave from Florida.

This worked out well for Wanda since she owned a luxurious condo in Fort Lauderdale. She had decided to offer Kirk employment with her as a chauffeur and companion. He realized that this would last only until she got tired of him.

"Wanda, dear, I really do appreciate your offer, and I've been carefully thinking about it, I have. But, you know, if I'm doing that, you might be getting tired of me and I'd need to be leaving. Then it could be very difficult for me to get back to working at what I'm doing now. So thinking better of it, I'm reluctantly saying no. I do hope you'll not be thinking ill of me for it," Kirk answered her politely. He did like *getting it on* with her; she was a very talented sexual partner.

"No, Kirk. I do understand although I love being with you. What if we do this: spend time with me whenever you can, vacations, days off, or if you happen to be in the States for some reason. I'll pay for your flights and any expenses, of course," Wanda offered hopefully. He was too good to let go of completely, and he preferred older women too.

"You have a deal, you dear sweetheart. Any time I can be getting away, I'll be right at your side or on top or however you want me. I don't want you being worried that I'm having no further interest, Wanda, because I'm greatly attracted to you in many ways."

"Oh, I'm so glad you feel that way, Kirk. Now come here, you handsome hunk of Irishman. I want to ravage you," she said and grabbed him hungrily.

* * *

The change of destination for the ship caused some unforeseen planning by Loretta and Edmund. They had intended to disembark in Biloxi, not Miami. Having Hunter along would require him being caged in the cargo section of any commercial aircraft. This was something they were unwilling to subject him to, no matter what. They thought about renting a car and driving back home, a distance of nearly two thousand miles.

"No, Larry promised us a plane to use when we went home. I'm going to call him right now," Edmund told Loretta emphatically.

"Hello, Larry, this is Edmund. There's been a change of plan here. Our ship needs to be repaired in Miami. They couldn't do it all in Bermuda, so we're stuck for transportation back home. Can you arrange for a plane to get us and Hunter back to Wyoming? We're still a couple of days out 'til we get to Florida."

"Sure, no problem. If you can just take a taxi over to the Opa-locka airfield, we can get you on a plane there. It's only about sixteen miles from Miami, and we have flights coming down there all the time. We'll fly you folks back to Casper. That's where your car is, right?" Larry offered.

"We sure appreciate it, Larry. Hate to think of driving all the way back, and we wouldn't put Hunter in a cage in a plane's baggage compartment. What day and time should we plan on being at Opa-locka?"

"I'll get right back with you as soon as I check on that," Larry assured them.

Two days later, as their ship docked at Port Everglades, everyone said their goodbyes. Loretta and Wanda promised to keep in touch, exchanging addresses and phone numbers. Hunter and Princess looked wistfully at each other as their humans walked down the gangplank and departed. Captain Demetriopoulos wished everyone

171

a safe trip home then turned to the urgent matter of getting his ship repaired.

The next afternoon, settled comfortably into their seats on the De Havilland Dash 8 with Hunter buckled in, they took off for home.

"Finally. The cruise was more than we'd bargained for wasn't it, Loretta?" Edmund asked her, smiling affectionately. She looked at him lovingly and nodded.

CHAPTER 38

Sheriff Looks for Clues

At about 10:30 p.m., they arrived back home, dead tired. Edmund dropped Loretta off at her house next door and pulled his car into the driveway of his. Hunter was eager to get out too. He ran up to the front door and began sniffing around. Edmund unlocked to front door and brought in his luggage. Then he poured out water for Hunter, who seemed more interested in sniffing around the house than anything else. He woofed a few times as he checked things out.

Not sure what attracted Hunter's attention, Edmund began looking around and noticed that a few things had been disturbed. Two drawers in the kitchen were open and had been rifled through. The liquor cabinet door was ajar too. Looking inside, he noticed that his bottle of Drambuie was gone. Perhaps in the haste to leave, he'd absentmindedly put it somewhere else. Glancing around the room, he didn't see it.

The phone rang, and Loretta was calling. She sounded uneasy. "Edmund, I think someone's been in my house. So many of my things have been disturbed, thrown around, and I'm sure some stuff is missing. Can you come over please?"

"Yes, of course, dear heart. You know, someone's been prowling around over here too," Edmund told her but calmly. "I'll be right there." Suddenly he remembered his stash of money in the basement.

Although very tired and his right leg throbbing, he hurried downstairs and pulled a medium-sized rock out of the basement wall. Behind it, the metal box was still there. He opened it, and fortunately, the money was safe inside. He breathed a sigh of relief. Unless somebody knew it was hidden there, they wouldn't look for loose foundation rocks. Then he and Hunter walked over to Loretta's place after tucking his pistol into his jacket pocket.

Loretta frantically hugged him when he got to the door. Hunter began sniffing around as he checked in each room.

"Have you heard any sounds?" Edmund asked. She shook her head no as they began checking for anything missing. A number of items had vanished including some cash she kept in a can on a cupboard shelf. An antique clock was gone and a set of silverware with the case.

"Did you say that someone broke into your house too, Edmund?" Loretta asked, concerned.

"I haven't had time to see how they got in yet, but let's look at your doors and windows right now."

His many years of investigative knowledge were beginning to kick in as they checked points of entry together. It had rained while they were away, and he observed large footprints outside the kitchen door and on the scuff mat.

"Be careful not to walk where the footprints are, dear, and don't touch any flat surfaces or handles if possible. Fingerprints, you know," he cautioned her. "We'll call the sheriff in the morning. Whoever was in here is long gone by now, and I'm just too tired to do any more tonight, aren't you?"

"Yes, I'm exhausted, Edmund. We can report it tomorrow. Will you stay here with me tonight? I'm shaken up and don't want to be alone now," she said, still frightened.

"Me too, dear love, and Hunter will be here too. We should try to rest and get to sleep now. I'll call Sheriff Vargas bright and early," he replied, hugging her warmly while stroking her hair. "I *am* curious how he got in. There aren't any broken doors or windows that I can see so far."

The next morning, the sheriff arrived about 8:30 a.m., shaking hands with Edmund and Loretta. They began looking over her house and soon found the latch on the basement bulkhead had been pried loose. He called his office and ordered a deputy to come over and take a plaster cast of the found footprints outside.

"You know, Ed, this is now the eighth burglary like this in just three weeks," he told Rambar. "We're starting to put together a picture of the MO. Seems like he or she listens to local gossip or just drives around these small towns looking for signs that people have gone away.

"It could be that he goes around posing as a salesman or maybe a survey taker. Whatever it is that he or she does, I'm sure they'll have a good cover story to explain their whereabouts. I've been checking with neighbors in case they may have noticed anything suspicious. Only a few strangers have moved into this area recently, but I'm checking on them too," Sheriff Vargas continued. "We'll find 'em eventually."

"Here's a list of what was taken from my place, Ralph, but I haven't gone through everything yet. There could be more. Loretta is trying to figure out what's gone right now," Edmund told the sheriff.

"By the way, Ed, you have an alarm system, don't you?"

"Just an infrared beam across my driveway, but I turned it off when we left. Nobody inside to monitor it when I'm gone. Hunter usually hears it and barks to alert me when we're home."

"Okay, let's see what they took," Vargas said as he looked over Ed's list. "I see they got your bottle of Drambuie. That's pretty low, isn't it? Taking a man's booze? I see they made off with your loose cash, an antique pocket watch, a briefcase, and a bunch of DVDs and CDs. He or she seemed to have had plenty of time to look around, probably the same over at Loretta's too."

"Funny, but I didn't notice any tire tracks last night. Because I was pretty tired, so I checked this morning. There were some in the driveway, but I ran over 'em, so they probably won't be of much help," Edmund lamented.

"Fingerprints are unlikely. I'm thinking our burglar probably wore gloves since we couldn't lift any prints at the other crime scenes. At one of the houses, we did get a fuzzy picture from the owner's surveillance camera. Somewhat indistinct though. Our culprit tried to stay in the shadows as much as possible," Vargas related.

"It looked like a well-dressed male, average height, and thin weight, between forty and sixty. He had on a hat so no way to see hair color. Couldn't determine if he was clean-shaven or not. It could possibly have even been a woman in men's clothing. It's not a lot to go on at this point, but we'll figure it out."

They walked over to Loretta's place, and she greeted them. More composed now, she offered a listing of things missing. Many were small antique items that meant a lot to her, as well as new electronic gear including her computer and printer.

"I found a pack of cigarettes in the living room, and neither Edmund nor I smoke," she presented it to Sheriff Vargas using a pen inside the open pack as she'd seen done on TV crime shows. It was a half-empty pack of Cavalier filter tips.

"Now that's impressive, Loretta. You and Ed here make quite a team, not like your average victims," Ralph told her, impressed. "Now I'm going over to your neighbors in case they saw something."

* * *

Being a rural town, the houses were spread out a hundred or so feet between them, not like in a city. The sheriff knocked on the door of the widow Henderson's house. She was home and came to the door quickly. A woman of seventy years, she was an observant person with much time to notice things. This is the type of witness police always like. They see everything and remember what they saw.

"Well, well, if it isn't Sheriff Vargas, you old so-and-so. Come on in here, and I'll get us some coffee. What brings you over to these parts?" she asked, happy to have a visitor.

"Your neighbors Ed and Loretta both had their houses burglarized while they were away. Did you happen to see anything suspicious in the last few days or so?" he began hopefully. Maybe something she saw might help.

"Well, you know I'm home most of the time since Fred died last year. A few days back, I did see a big dark car, maybe black, pull into Ed's driveway. It was like a, what do you call 'em, an SUV, and it stayed there quite a while, 'bout an hour. Then it took off. I considered that maybe Ed and Loretta got home, and they had somebody visiting 'em," she told him.

Immediately interested, the sheriff asked, "Did you see anything else, like who was driving it, a man or a woman, and could you see what they were wearing?"

"It's too far over there to see much, but it looked like a man to me, and he had on some real dark clothes. I think it was like a long coat. I saw him traipse around the house a couple times, outside before he went around to the back," she continued.

"Do you happen to recall what day it was?" he probed in a friendly manner.

"Well, let's see. It was in the afternoon, probably around two, and I'm tryin' to think what day it was. I had a doctor's appointment the next day, on Tuesday, so I got my car out of the garage and that's when I noticed the SUV over there. It would have been on Monday. Yup, a Monday, for sure."

"You've been very helpful, Mrs. Henderson. You sure have, and I genuinely appreciate your assistance. Oh, and thank you for your good coffee too. I needed a lift this morning," he told her sincerely. Now he had more to go on. Not a lot more, but it was something. In an area full of white vehicles, not too many others were dark colored.

I wonder how many of the newcomers to this area drive dark SUVs, and how many are likely to wear long black, or at least, dark coats? he thought.

CHAPTER 39

Catching the Burglar

After considerable efforts, Sheriff Vargas found that, of recent arrivals in the area, only three drove dark-colored SUVs. One was owned by a young couple with two infant children, both under three years old. Another was driven by a Catholic priest and furnished by his parish. The third vehicle was owned by the man who'd opened a new mortuary, one Obadiah Pulcher.

A number of area residents had seen him going door-to-door, passing out leaflets and visiting people when he found them home. If no one answered the buzzer, he would sometimes try the back door, carefully using his gloved hand. When a few of the houses were close to each other, he'd leave without entering. Those at some distance from neighbors were his choice targets.

Usually he knew immediately whether or not a particular home would be worth prowling through. If the furnishings were shabby or the place revealed sloppy or nonexistent housekeeping, he would go onto the next one that showed promise. If he heard a dog barking, he'd simply leave a leaflet in the doorway and depart.

* * *

By the fourth week, three more homes had been burglarized. Vargas had a hunch and decided that it could be worthwhile to check up on the new mortician.

He contacted the State Mortuary Society in Cheyenne. They had no record of anyone by the name of Obadiah S. E. Pulcher being a member or having a licensed funeral home in Wyoming. Now he was deciding how to flush out this individual without spooking him into bolting and leaving the cases unsolved.

Knowing Edmund's background, he visited him again, and they discussed how to best tackle the investigation.

"As you know, Ralph, most of my work dealt with espionage and counter intelligence. However, I did a lot of undercover stuff too and maybe that could be useful here. What if I were to see this guy about prearranging a funeral for myself? He could possibly know my name since he was already in my house, so I'd use a fake one, of course."

"You know I'd really appreciate the help, Ed, if you'd feel like doing it," Vergas said, glad for Edmund's possible assistance. "I've got a real small transmitter you could carry in your shirt pocket, and it'll pick up any conversation or sounds within about twenty feet. It could be handy to have, just in case."

The next morning, Edmund, Loretta, and Hunter drove over to the mortuary. She dropped him and their dog off at the door of the establishment. With his dark glasses, white cane, and nondescript clothing, they walked in the front door. Waiting inside, Mr. Pulcher greeted them with affected warmness.

"Ah, good morning, sir. How are you today? My, what a pretty doggie. What may I do for you this fine, sunny day?"

"Hello, are you the man I talk to about planning a funeral in advance?" Edmund asked, seemingly confused.

"Yes indeed, dear sir. You've come to the right place. My name is Obadiah Pulcher. I'm the mortuary director. You are interested in a preneed plan, is that right?"

"Well, my friend Ernie died recently, as you know since your funeral home handled the service, and it got me thinking. I'm not getting any younger and decided I'd better get this taken care of while I'm still kicking. Don't want to leave a big mess for my relatives," Edmund said convincingly.

"Yes, I understand, and that's very wise of you. We offer a variety of preneed plans for our clients. What is your name please?"

"Oh, I'm Fred Caspersen. Pleased to make your acquaintance," Edmund said, extending his hand into midair.

Pulcher noticed the handshake attempt and gripped it warmly with both his hands while thinking, *Got another sucker, and this one doesn't even need any immediate efforts.* Rubbing his hands together, he inquired, "Are you thinking of paying for the prearrangements immediately or in payments?"

"I might just as well get it paid for right off. I've got the money, and I hate to have bills dragging on," Edmund offered enticingly.

Dollar signs flashed in front of Pulcher's eyes as he described the various options in caskets, floral arrangements, burial clothes, a grave plot, and other professional services.

Hunter had been sniffing around the room as well as by Pulcher's feet. Edmund didn't want the mortician to become annoyed by the dog's attention. He then thought of a distraction.

"All this talk has me feeling depressed. I could sure use a drink of something strong about now. Would you happen to have a bottle of anything handy, Mr. Pulcher?"

"Well now, let me see, Mr. Caspersen. We do want to please our clients. I just happen to have a bottle of liqueur around here somewhere. Do you like Drambuie, sir?"

"Can't say I've ever tried it. Pretty fancy stuff, I'd guess. Well, let's have some," Edmund said innocently.

Pulcher found two glasses and poured the drinks. Hunter had disappeared unnoticed behind a doorway curtain into the next room. Handing the glass to Edmund, Pulcher noticed the dog emerge from the back holding a briefcase. It was the one he'd stolen from this man's house, but he didn't know that it was. Hunter resisted letting it go and resisted fiercely.

"What does my dog have there, Mr. Pulcher? He likes to pick up things sometimes."

"It's…it's just an old shoe that I had in the back," the mortician said nervously, trying to pull it away from the animal.

"That's odd. It looks like my briefcase, Mr. Pulcher. Oh, and we've been drinking *my* Drambuie too," Edmund said accusingly, taking off his dark glasses.

"Why, how could you know that…," Pulcher said, looking startled. Then he realized that this man in front of him could see perfectly. He wasn't blind at all.

"Oh, I'm…I'm sure you're mistaken, Mr. Caspersen. I didn't realize you could see, and…and…" His voice trailed off. He turned toward the front door.

Sheriff Vargas had been listening to everything through the transmitter he'd given Edmund and barged in suddenly. It caught Pulcher completely off guard.

"You are under arrest, Mr. Pulcher, for suspicion of burglary," Vargas told him firmly while slapping handcuffs onto his wrists. Based on the sheriff's word, the local magistrate had issued a search warrant for the premises.

After having one of his deputies take Pulcher away, Vargas and Edmund began searching for other stolen loot. It soon became obvious that the mortician had been sleeping in the back room on a cot. He had stashed all the things he stole in there too.

Over the next few hours, they identified many of the items listed in the burglary reports and carefully labeled them. He had Edmund sign as a witness to the chain of custody and took everything over to the jail vault.

With the mortician locked up, no further burglaries were reported. Apparently, his was a solo act with no accomplices.

"We can certainly thank Hunter for wrapping up this case quickly," Vargas said, patting the dog gratefully. "We better get him something special for his fine work. Don't you think, Edmund?"

Loretta returned and came inside. "I saw a deputy putting someone into a patrol car. What have you been up to now, you naughty boy?" she asked Edmund jokingly. "And you too, Ralph. Did you catch a criminal or something?" she teased, knowing all along what they were doing.

"In fact, we did, with Edmund's and Hunter's great help. You'll get most all of your stuff back soon. It was this new mortician who

was taking stuff around here. Oh yeah, we found some Cavalier cigarettes in his coat too, the same kind you found at your place. He's
gonna go away for a long time."

Several weeks later, after being held in custody as a possible
flight risk, Obadiah Pulcher was put on trial. Along with discover-
ing his real name, he was alleged to have assaulted and robbed a gas
station attendant in a nearby town. Thus, he faced charges for that
crime along with burglary and fencing stolen property.

The presiding judge, a man with a wry sense of humor himself,
commented on the clever alias the defendant had invented. Then
once proven guilty, he *threw the book* at him. Sentenced to eighteen
years, he was incarcerated in the state prison at Rawlins. He was mur-
dered four years later in a brawl with two other inmates.

CHAPTER 40

Wedding Plans

"Loretta, dear, this is Wanda. I have some wonderful news. Kirk has been transferred back to London from Gibraltar. I'm buying a townhouse there, in Knightsbridge near Harrods. You see, we're going to get married, and I'm so happy that I could nearly burst."

"Oh my goodness, Wanda. This is so sudden, but I'm very, very happy for you both. Have you thought it through carefully? I don't mean to throw cold water on your plans, but how can I put this delicately? There is a considerable difference in your ages, dear heart. I wouldn't want to see you got hurt later on."

"I know, dear Loretta, I am twenty-three years older than Kirk, but we've discussed this over and over again. Kirk couldn't be more devoted to me, and you must see the beautiful engagement ring he gave me. After all, you and Edmund are several years apart in age too, aren't you?"

"You're right, Wanda. Love doesn't take age into consideration, does it? Did I show you *my* engagement ring? Edmund and I picked it out together."

"It's all so wonderful. It really is. But the real reason I called is that with me moving to London, it will be terribly hard on dear Princess. Because she and Hunter like each other so very much, would you be willing to take her permanently? I know it's a lot to ask."

"I know that Edmund likes her very much, and Hunter would be overjoyed to be with her again. I'm sure that we can take her. Between both of our places, there is plenty of room for them to run around and play. Yes, we can definitely give her a good new home. It's like having two wonderful children and at our ages too.

"We're planning on getting married about two weeks from now and have invited only a few people to it. There will be Nigel and Dorris, who are going to be on vacation. Then Larry and Chanthini, both CIA people, and a few local friends. We're going to have a civil wedding, using a justice of the peace, not a preacher.

"On my first wedding, I didn't have a chance to wear a wedding gown because we couldn't afford much of anything. This time, I'm going to indulge myself and walk down the aisle and everything. Edmund agrees. His former wife has been gone for many years, and they couldn't afford a formal wedding either.

"If you and, hopefully, Kirk, can arrange to bring Princess up here by then, we'd love to have you both here to help us celebrate. Do talk with Kirk and see if you can, okay?" Loretta told her excitedly.

After getting off the phone, Loretta found Edmund outside. "I have something wonderful to tell you. We're going to be parents of another fur baby. Wanda called and she'd like us to take Princess. She's marrying Kirk, moving to London, and feels that it would be too difficult on her dog. What do you think, Edmund?"

"I think that would be splendid, Loretta. Hunter will be so happy to have the love of his life back with him again, forever. When will Wanda bring her up here, or do we have to go and get her?"

"She's trying to arrange their schedules so that Kirk can be here too. I told her that we're planning on about two weeks for our wedding. I do hope they can make it, don't you?"

* * *

During the next few days, Loretta was busy making all the plans. They decided to have their nuptials in the huge backyard at her place, provided the weather would be good. There were many things to arrange for, but her sister arrived from Laramie to help.

Edmund reluctantly decided to invite his son and daughter-in-law to come up for the ceremony. They declined, pleading too many things going on in Arizona for them to get away. His son, Bob, asked, not too discreetly, if the pending marriage would affect Edmund's will and other legal matters. Assuring his greedy adult child that he would still be the primary beneficiary if Edmund would passed on, Bob felt much relieved. Nevertheless, Edmund had changed his will to provide Loretta with a substantial portion of his estate and act as his executor.

Receiving Edmund's call and invitation, Larry asked if he had even been in Israel. Immediately, Rambar knew what his friend was up to. "I hope you're not offering me another assignment, Larry. You know that now I am officially retired from anything more, no more courier runs, nothing. However, I am still available to consult with you and a few other colleagues about security related matters, but nothing more. So come up to our wedding and enjoy a day off from all the cloak and dagger stuff, okay?"

"Of course, I understand, Edmund, but I've already talked with Nigel Brown at MI6. He told me that his wife and he, along with one of his people, Kirk Hanrahan, will be present at your festivities too. I heard that Chanthini from our Denver office is coming too, so it'll be sort of like *old home week*, won't it?"

"To be frank about it, Larry, it's starting to sound more like a mini summit, but we'll see how it goes. And no, I've never been to Israel," Edmund responded with a strong feeling of suspicion.

That afternoon, Edmund, Loretta, and Hunter took a long walk along a pathway that wound its way around the town perimeter.

"I'm so excited about everything that I can hardly get it organized, Edmund. Later, after the wedding is done with and we're fully rested, would you like to go somewhere for our honeymoon? I've thought for many, many years that I'd love to see the pyramids, the sphinx, and the ruins in Egypt. I don't mean on some long cruise. I'm kind of burned out on that, but just a flight over there and back. Do you think that might be something of interest, Edmund?"

"I've never been there either, but it has fascinated me for a long time. I could see us stopping off in Israel for a couple of days too, if you'd be interested in going there," Edmund said, having second thoughts about dismissing Larry's offer so quickly.

"Well, since we're in that area anyway, I'd kind of like seeing some of the holy places where Jesus lived and taught. Only about two weeks though. I don't want to be gone so long as before now that it's getting into late fall," Loretta thought aloud.

When they returned home, Edmund walked back to his house with Hunter, then called Larry. "I dismissed your offer too quickly, Larry. Tell me what the agency has in mind and what kind of incentive are they offering?"

"You're still talking to me on your secure phone, aren't you, Edmund?" Larry asked, not doubting his friend's long experience. "With Nigel, Kirk, and Chanthini coming there for your wedding, we can fill in all the details then. What I can tell you is this: the perks will be the same as your London courier assignment, but you will be accompanied by both American and British shadows until the information is safely dropped off with the Mossad in Tel Aviv. Sound interesting?"

"Perhaps, provided that it can also be a honeymoon trip for Loretta and me, all expenses paid, naturally," Edmund responded with modest interest.

"There is some degree of urgency about it, so you'd definitely make your first stop in Israel, then wherever you want to go after that is up to you and Loretta."

"Okay, Larry. I'll think seriously about it," Edmund replied but was still not committed.

CHAPTER 41

A Courier Once Again

As Edmund and Loretta watched, a private plane landed smoothly at the Casper airport. Wanda emerged holding Princess's leash, followed by Kirk carrying three pieces of luggage. She saw them waiting by the runway fence and waved excitedly. Her dog barked a friendly greeting upon seeing them. Kirk gave them a *thumbs up* signal and smiled.

In the terminal building, Wanda hugged Loretta warmly. "I am ashamed because I was so excited over our wedding that I forgot to congratulate you and Edmund. We are definitely going to be here. We wouldn't miss it for the world. Kirk and I will take our vows in the UK because it will help me to get my dual citizenship. Otherwise, we would love to have made it a double ceremony with you two."

After the drive over to Loretta's and Edmund's homes about seventy miles from Casper, Princess and Hunter were reunited. It brought tears to the women's eyes. Both animals yelped happily, pawed at, and embraced each other with their front paws while furiously licking each other's face.

After a home-cooked meal at Loretta's, the two men wandered around outside, smoking and discussing the possible assignment to Israel.

"As a well-known singer once said, 'Life gets very precious when there's less of it to waste,'" Edmund began. "Still, someone else said that 'you can never be too thin or too rich.' I am seriously thinking about doing it because Loretta wants to go to Egypt for our honeymoon, and I've suggested adding Israel to the itinerary. She wants to see the holy sites in Jerusalem if we go there. It's only about forty or fifty miles over there from Tel Aviv. If Wanda comes along, the women could take an American Express day tour there while you and I meet with the Mossad."

"Sure now, it sounds good. I'm pretty sure that I'll be one of your shadows on this wee adventure, along with one or two of your people. When Nigel gets himself here, I can be confirming that for you. You can be sure there will be another two or more fine souls watching us as well. I do enjoy working these operations with you, sir," Kirk replied with anticipation. "You know, I've never been to Israel myself."

* * *

Hunter and Princess happily romped all over the expansive grounds of both places. The second afternoon, he spotted a young rattlesnake close to Princess and shook it to death before it could strike. She examined it carefully, never having seen one before but refrained from taking a bite out of it after a warning growl from Hunter.

Edmund and Kirk drove back over to the Casper airport to pick up Nigel and Dorris who had arrived from London via Denver and then had taken the shuttle up from there.

Larry and Chanthini drove up from Colorado to be a part of the festivities. Princess became the flower girl and Hunter was the ring bearer. Loretta's sister and Wanda were the maids of honor, with Nigel as the best man. It was a double-ring ceremony. A few local folks were also invited including the widow Mrs. Henderson from next door.

Somewhat anxious to get back to Washington (Langley), Larry had flown to Denver and picked up Chanthini the next morning. Accompanied by two or more undercover types, he had been given the intelligence-embedded ring for Edmund. It was a hunch, but Larry was sure that Edmund would take on the easy courier assignment.

After the ceremony and reception, Loretta and her new husband, Edmund, had a chance to be alone and talk.

"Larry offered me an opportunity to have our entire honeymoon trip paid for by my former agency. I just have to drop off some information for the Israeli government when we arrive. That's all, nothing to take back. Would you mind if I played courier on the way to Egypt?" Edmund asked her nonchalantly

"Well, we did spend quite a lot of money on our fancy wedding. It would be practical having the trip paid for, wouldn't it? But are you sure it would be safe? I don't want to lose you for anything," Loretta replied, looking serious.

"It wouldn't be any more hazardous than just going to the Middle East in the first place. I'll have escorts from both the CIA, MI6, and the Israelis. Kirk will be with us too. The Israelis are damned good at protecting whatever they're involved in. That's one reason we're flying over there on El Al Airline. It's probably the most well-protected carrier in the business," Edmund reassured her.

"I think it will be okay. I do have a good feeling about it, don't you?"

"Yes, dear love, I really do. With Wanda coming too, we'll just be four tourists seeing the world, invisible to anyone out to cause trouble," he said back confidently. "The only thing is that we will need to start out within the next few days. Can we be ready by then?"

"To get a paid honeymoon like that, I'm sure we can be ready by Thursday. That's three days from now. My sister loves our dogs, and she said that she'll be happy to stay with them while we're gone. I told her it'll only be about a week or maybe ten days. Does that sound about right, Edmund?"

"Yeah, I think that nails it. We can be home before any snow gets here, I think. We can fly out of Casper to Denver. I think Wanda and Kirk might like to do a little sightseeing there. I'd feel a lot more rested if we spent the night in the *Mile High City* before going on to New York then Tel Aviv."

With Kirk along, Rambar found Larry and took the ring. It still fit firmly onto his finger. From this minute on, he would be under unobtrusive, but close, surveillance until he and the others reached the authorities in Israel.

CHAPTER 42

Playing the Godfather

Arriving at JFK Airport, with two or perhaps even more CIA shadows watching over them, as well as Kirk and a pair of British agents, they all settled in to await the El Al flight to Tel Aviv. Boarding would not begin for three hours, so Kirk and Wanda decided to look in a few of the various shops.

Loretta suggested she and Edmund step outside for some fresh air. They found a somewhat vacant spot to watch planes taking off and landing. Most other travelers had opted to watch from inside the terminal, so they were alone at that location.

They had only been standing there for a few minutes when two men approached them, thinking that the well-dressed elderly couple would be easy pickings. "Hand over your wallet, old man, and your purse too, lady. We don't want to rough you up, so fork 'em over, NOW!"

Ever resourceful, Edmund glared at them with feigned anger. "Hey, whatsa matter wit' you lousy punks, eh? You think you gonna just stick up some old'a people right here inna th' airport?" he shouted in a gravelly voice while affecting an Italian accent.

"Do you punks know who I am, huh? I'ma Edmundo Rambarini. That'sa *Don* Rambarini to you, an' this is'a Valentina Scaradelli. They know us big in Chicago. Now I'ma gonna tell you, get th' hell out of here an' I'ma mean the whole damm'a airport, or you gonna be sleepin' with the fishes tonight. Capeech?"

At that moment, Kirk and Wanda saw what looked like trouble happening to Loretta and Edmund a short distance away. Kirk told Wanda to stay a little way back as he hurried toward them.

Edmund told the muggers in a loud voice, "Here'sa come one a' my boys right now, you punks."

They looked around to see this dark-haired wiry young man running toward them. Both looked at each other and panicked.

Ever alert, Kirk immediately picked up on the situation. "Mr. Rambar, sir, would these two be bothering you now?"

The would-be robbers were even more alarmed by hearing Kirk's Irish brogue. He must be a capo from a Dutch/Irish mob.

"Ah, is just'a two punks tryin' ta' be the big men. Let 'em know we don'ta like their company, Kirk. Give'a them a little souvenir to remember us, eh?"

"Yes, sir, whatever you'd be liking." With that, he rammed his right knee into one of the men's crotch, hard. The man, now looking seriously scared, crumpled to the floor. The second one started backing up as Kirk approached him menacingly. With a swift karate chop, he hit the man's nose, breaking it. Blood oozed out onto his jacket and a knife dropped out of the pocket, clanking as it hit the concrete.

"We think you'd best be going now while you still can," Kirk warned them as the bloodied one helped the first man to his feet. They took off limping away.

"Are you both all right, Edmund, Loretta? Is your ring still safe too?" Kirk asked, genuinely concerned about them. Unknown to them, two strangers watched from a distance but didn't intervene.

"Yes, of course, Kirk. I was just about to take them both *on* when you spoiled my fun, but we do thank you most sincerely," Edmund joked but grateful.

"Edmund, dear, you never cease to amaze me. I was petrified with fear that they were going to kill us or something," Loretta told him, still shaken. "How did you think to come up with that voice and everything? You made a better mafia *don* than Marlon Brando did in *The Godfather*. Just amazing."

"Aye, he's truly an amazing man, and you're lucky to have him as your husband, very lucky indeed," Kirk assured her and motioned to Wanda that it was safe to join them. After seeing Kirk in action, she was even *more* turned on by him, and lustful thoughts filled her head.

After having some afternoon tea, they boarded the El Al plane to Israel and were hopeful of no further adventures. The flight to Tel Aviv was long and without incident but comfortable. Loretta and Edmund napped much of the way.

The plane landed smoothly at Ben Gurion International Airport. As they all disembarked, Kirk and Edmund both felt they recognized one of two men who had been seated close to them. These were both Mossad operatives assigned to watch over Rambar and the intelligence-filled ring. They had been on the planes all the way from Denver and could now escort Edmund and Kirk to their head-quarters at a secret location somewhere near the Knesset parliament building. First, though, it was important to get the group settled into their hotel.

Nevertheless, as soon as Loretta and Edmund had unpacked and relaxed a little, there was a knock on their door. Kirk and the two Mossad agents came in.

"We dislike disturbing you so soon, Mr. Rambar. However, we must escort you and Mr. Hanrahan to our office immediately. I'm sure you will understand, and it will only take a short time out of your holiday," the one agent told Edmund. He turned toward Loretta and assured her, "This is government business, and we'll have them back with you ladies before dinner time, I promise."

Although exhausted, Rambar fully understood. He was just as eager to get rid of the intelligence-bearing ring as the Israeli government officials were to have it. The four departed in an unmarked vehicle and arrived at the Mossad offices within ten minutes.

Ushered into a secure, soundproof office, the officer in charge greeted them cordially. "We are aware of your excellent professional reputation, Mr. Rambar, and we are most grateful to you for bringing us this most important, even vital, intelligence.

"Mr. Hanrahan, you also have our sincere gratitude for safe-guarding Mr. Rambar during his trip over here. Our operatives kept us informed of your quick thinking and physical abilities at those critical moments in New York. He and the American government owe you a great deal as well."

With the ring safely in Israeli hands, the Mossad OIC again offered them his gratitude. "Now that you are in our little country, I hope that we can assist you in enjoying the many sights available. How can we help you right now?"

"Our women are hoping to do a tour over to Jerusalem very soon, perhaps tomorrow. They'll see the American Express people and arrange it as soon as they're rested. Frankly, I'm concerned about their safety. What could your agency do to keep them out of harm's way? We'd both be most grateful for whatever assistance you might provide, wouldn't we, Kirk?" Rambar said, glancing toward him.

The younger man looked sincerely fearful and nodded his agreement.

"As you can imagine, we highly value your efforts toward ensuring the security of Israel and will not allow any unfortunate incident to you and your party to lessen your enjoyment of our country. We will provide a discreet but close surveillance of your ladies while they tour Jerusalem. They will be protected," the OIC assured them. "Now you must be exhausted from your trip. We'll drive you back to your hotel, so you can recover."

* * *

Going eastbound, most travelers find that jet lag is more severe than going west. Even while suffering it, the women wanted to see Jerusalem and boarded a tour bus in the early afternoon. They arrived in the Old City about 3:00 p.m., stopping first at the Dome of the Rock, then walked the Via Dolorosa.

The weather was warm and pleasant as they stopped for refreshments. Then they took in the other important sites for the next two hours and reboarded their tour bus at 6:30 p.m. Just outside the historic part of the city, the bus stopped abruptly, and the guide ordered everyone to get out.

They were all ushered away from the vehicle about a hundred feet while Israeli police and soldiers cordoned it off. A few minutes later, there was a huge explosion, and the bus was engulfed in flames. Metal parts flew everywhere as the gas tank exploded just seconds after the initial explosion.

People screamed, and Wanda, showing great presence of mind, took pictures of it and a few videos showing the crowd's reaction. Loretta tried to comfort a few of the elderly passengers, and a nearby restaurant brought out bottles of water for everyone. By now, photographers were taking videos from a distance while the fire still burning.

After taking witnesses' statements, the police escorted the passengers over to a waiting bus that had just arrived. They returned to Tel Aviv without incident but accompanied by motorcycle officers. Loretta and Wanda hurried into the hotel and saw Kirk and Edmund in the lobby having a cool drink. They ran over to the men and excitedly related what had almost happened to them.

Wanda hugged Kirk tightly, relieved to be back in his arms and safety. Loretta did the same with Edmund, accidentally spilling his drink in her haste to embrace him.

"Oh, it was a frightening experience, dear, dear Edmund. We were just minutes from being killed. I'm so scared. Could we leave for Egypt as soon as possible?" Loretta pleaded.

Wanda concurred, looking at Kirk with fearful eyes. Both men agreed since the courier duty was completed, there was little reason to stay any longer. Edmund and Kirk had strolled around Tel Aviv and even bought a few souvenirs for the women. Everyone was ready to go. Able to get on an Egyptair flight, they departed at 6:00 p.m. for the short trip to Cairo.

CHAPTER 43

A Coup in Cairo

Although the day's heat had lessened into a moderately cool evening, the city was restless. There was an eerie feeling, just under the surface, in the crowded streets. Edmund and his party checked into a centrally located hotel, then proceeded down to the dining room for a light dinner. After eating, they went outside to view the surrounding city at night.

Deciding on a stroll through the market stands and shops, the women found a few miniature sphinx statues and pictures of Egyptian gods, Nefertiti, and cats with hieroglyphic writing on each of them. With few European tourists out and about, some of the locals eyed them suspiciously.

They located the nearby American Express office, which had closed by now. In the morning, they would make reservations for a day trip out to the pyramids and other historic sites. After separating from the men in Israel, both Loretta and Wanda had firmly determined to stay close to their men while sightseeing. Kirk and Edmund agreed this to be a wise course to follow.

After an ample croissant breakfast on the hotel terrace, they booked a tour to see the sphinx and pyramids. Fortunately, there were places available for the late morning departure. Later, the Cairo Historical Museum would be on the schedule.

It would be a long day for the elderly Edmund, who had purchased a cane last night in the market. By checking in with the American consulate for routine security reasons, he was able to wran-

195

gle an invitation to an embassy party. He knew a few of the people there from the old days, many of whom had worked for various other government agencies. The soiree was to begin at eighty thirty the next evening, and Edmund was graciously invited to bring along his wife and other guests.

Kirk also contacted the British consulate for the same security concerns. As a junior member of MI6, he had a few contacts within the diplomatic corps and was merely registered as a tourist visitor to the Egyptian capital. Somewhat miffed, he had hoped to meet with security officials at the embassy, but no offer was extended.

The tour bus was air conditioned, and Edmund opted to only look at or walk briefly around the historic monuments. He would then return to the pleasantly cool vehicle. Kirk escorted the women around the sites while they took a multitude of pictures. In good physical condition, he climbed way up on the Great Pyramid so Wanda could take photos of him from below.

After the strenuous tour, they settled in for refreshments near the museum. After hours of walking through the thousands of exhibits, they arrived at the gift shop. Edmund, always planning for eventualities, bought the women each a burka as souvenirs. If political conditions turned unfavorable, they could pass as Muslims. Kirk and he could disguise themselves as Middle Eastern men using Edmund's ever-present kit to modify their appearance.

They arrived at the American Embassy at 9:00 p.m. and were welcomed by the chargé d'affaires whom Edmund knew from past decades. He introduced them to various dignitaries, most of them strangers but cordial. After having a drink, listening to a welcoming speech by the ambassador, and staying a proper amount of time, they prepared to depart.

"Please, may we have your attention everyone?" an embassy staffer asked, sounding urgent. "We have just been informed that a military coup is in progress at this moment. We are concerned that there may be violent protests in the streets very soon. Therefore, we must advise those who are here to do one of two things. You may remain with us here on the embassy grounds. As you know, this is extraterritorial American soil and protected by members of the US Marine Corps.

"Your second option is to depart quickly and go to your hotels or to other embassies, but try to leave Cairo and Egypt by plane if possible. We do not feel it advisable to offer US government-marked staff cars as these may become targets for rioters. A limited number of local taxicabs are under contract to us for auxiliary transportation. The operators of these vehicles have been vetted thoroughly, are safe, and will transport you to wherever you need to go. Thank you, and we urge you to leave immediately."

Edmund, Kirk, and both women looked at each other, concerned but not panicked.

"We could go over to the British Embassy," Kirk offered. "But the rioters would be as likely to attack there as well."

"Let's get back to our hotel, grab our things, and get out to the airport. If you and Wanda could put on those new burkas while Kirk and I try to look more Middle Eastern, it could keep us a bit safer, I think," Edmund directed calmly.

They got on one of the secure cabs and drove back to their hotel, unharassed. Fifteen minutes later, they were each ready. The men had darkened their faces and put on conservative suits to wear. In his kit, Edmund had two small Red Crescent lapel pins to wear. He provided the women with some of the skin-darkening cream for their hands and around their eyes.

They were ready and got hurried with their luggage down to the waiting taxi. En route to the airport, crowds were already filling the main streets. As they went by, some of the excited local people peered into the car. Seeing what they took to be Egyptians inside, they let them pass, unchecked.

At the airport check-in counter, they attempted to get tickets for a departing British Airways flight to London or Paris or even Rome.

"I'm frightfully sorry, but those planes are fully booked for this flight, even the next one. Perhaps you might consider some other destination, Athens or Malta?" the polite but hurried agent asked quickly, hoping for an immediate reply.

"Let's go to Malta, everyone. We can more likely be getting a plane to London from there, I think," Kirk suggested. Edmund agreed after looking at the women who nodded.

Issued tickets and boarding passes, they arrived at the immigration control officer, who looked confused at seeing their British and American passports with their odd appearance. But with a long line of passengers impatient to board planes, he shrugged his shoulders and stamped their exit documents.

They practically ran out to the waiting aircraft even as the ground crew were starting to pull the boarding stairs away. When they saw the last-minute arrivals hurrying over to the plane, they pushed them back into place. Loretta and Wanda boarded first, followed by a badly limping Edmund, struggling with a heavy suitcase. Although the women also each carried a bag, Kirk followed, toting most of their luggage up into the plane just before the door was secured. They sat back in their seats, exhausted but safe.

CHAPTER 44

Returning Home

Arriving in Malta about two hours later at nearly 2:00 a.m., after dozing on the plane, they learned that the next flight to London would be six hours later. Not wanting to wait around the airport for that long, they decided to take a taxi into Valetta, have breakfast, and look around. Edmund had heard that the restaurant in the Hotel Phoenicia served excellent meals, so they went there. After a wonderful repast, they felt somewhat refreshed. The women and Kirk walked along the medieval battlements built by the knights of Malta. Edmund opted to rest nearby.

Finally able to board the London-bound plane, they flew over Elba, Napoleon's first place of banishment, and then over the Alps. They landed at Gatwick Airport in late morning, and a short train ride took them into Central London.

At The Dorchester hotel, a smiling older desk clerk looked up and greeted the new guests. He studied Edmund and told him, "It's an odd coincidence, sir, but you bear the most striking resemblance to a guest who stayed with us some months ago, a Lord Chesterton-Rancourt. A fine English gentleman he was too. By any chance, are you perhaps related to him, sir?"

"No, not unless he was an American. I don't know any relatives here. Well, there was my young nephew, but he doesn't live in London anymore," Edmund replied, quite tired and wanting to lie down for a while.

In their adjoining room, Wanda settled in and Kirk decided to give Nigel a call. After a short catch-up conversation, all four were invited for dinner the next evening. Kirk knocked on the door connecting their room with the Rambars and told them about Nigel's dinner invitation.

* * *

The Browns owned a tidy and spacious flat in Knightsbridge, a few blocks from Harrods. This location caused both Loretta and Wanda to be greatly interested. They knew that it was arguably the best department store in Europe, and they were determined to experience it and *buy* things.

During late afternoon cocktails at Dorris and Nigel's, the women mentioned that they'd taken the tour bus around London and how delighted they were to see it. Wanda told everyone that she was buying a flat nearby for her and Kirk. With that, the Browns offered them an open invitation to visit whenever Kirk was back from an assignment. Such was his job, to often be away from both city and country but mostly from Wanda. Nigel felt somewhat paternal toward Kirk, whom he liked very much for his intelligence and ability.

Curious about what had happened with his nephew Patric, Edmund took Nigel aside and quietly asked if he could check into it for him. He graciously obliged and learned that Patric was still in prison in the Midlands, with many years yet to serve out his sentence.

"He never tried to contact me," Edmund replied fatalistically. "And I've not tried to. I'm pleased that I was able to help prevent a terrible thing from happening."

They rejoined the other guests, and Wanda asked Loretta if she and Edmund could remain in the UK for a few more days.

"You see, Kirk and I would love to have you at our wedding. We can arrange to do it in just two or three days, a simple ceremony with only a few guests. Can you two stay in London that long? It would mean so much to us. Kirk has to get back to work soon, but we will take our honeymoon trip in a few months."

"I'm sure we can. We'd love to be here for you both," Loretta told her, smiling. "After all, you were there for ours." She looked over to Edmund, who had been following the conversation, and he weakly nodded his agreement.

Over dinner, Nigel, seated across from Rambar, said, "Do forgive me for mentioning it, Edmund, but you look quite unwell. You must be exhausted, aren't you?"

Edmund nodded again, even with less strength.

"Dorris and I spoke about it and would very much like for you and Loretta to spend a few days here as our guests. We have sufficient room, and you could relax out on our terrace when you feel better. Please accept our invitation. We would love to have you both," Nigel offered, trying not to show his very real concern about Edmund's condition.

"Thank you so much, Nigel. I think we need to accept your offer. I really must lie down for a while now, if you don't mind," Edmund replied gratefully.

He tried to get up but collapsed back in his chair. With his host holding one arm and Loretta on the other, they got him to the guest room, and he fell onto the bed with a groan.

"I'll have our physician come over and check on him straight away," Dorris told Loretta consolingly.

Less than two hours later, Dr. Corbett arrived, examined Rambar, then gave him an injection of vitamin B12 and some tablets.

"I suspect that Mr. Rambar has been overdoing it for a man his age, hasn't he?" With a reassuring smile toward Loretta, he proclaimed firmly, "Do not be unduly concerned. Your husband will be all right once his strength returns. But he should rest for a few days and then only moderate exercise until he has fully recovered."

"Of course he will, doctor. Thank you so much for coming over so quickly," Loretta offered with total gratitude, tears coming down her cheeks.

"Ah, you're a tough old bird, sir, and you're going to be fine in a short while, but no more young man heroics. Leave that to me, understand, sir?" Kirk told Edmund with feigned sternness.

The doctor departed along with the others, leaving Loretta and Edmund to go to bed. In her nightgown, relieved but still with tears in her eyes, she lay next to her husband. He put his arm around her shoulders with unexpected strength.

"Everything will be all right, dear love. We'll be back home soon, and we won't go anywhere again for a long, long time. I love you too much to die on you now. Don't worry, we're going to be okay. Now let's rest. We have a lot more living to do yet," Edmund whispered to her.

In the morning, Loretta checked them out of The Dorchester hotel. Wanda kept her room there until the wedding when she and Kirk could begin moving into the luxurious flat they'd picked out.

By the next day, Edmund was able to get up on his own and walk out to the sun-drenched terrace for coffee and a light meal. Loretta was with him, cautiously optimistic. His color was better, and he joked quietly with her as they held hands. Wanda arrived bringing flowers and cheery conversation. From work, Kirk called his best wishes and told Edmund he needed to be well enough for the wedding or Wanda would probably never forgive him.

In deference to Edmund's temporary condition, they postponed their wedding until the following week. They decided to take their vows at a small chapel near the Browns' home and have a small reception there with Dorris and Nigel as hosts.

On the fourth day, Edmund had shown remarkable improvement and walked with Loretta and Dorris over to a nearby park. They saw a few dogs enjoying their outing and frolicking in the open-run area with their owners.

"How I miss our dogs, Loretta. Let's plan on going home right after the wedding, if the doctor says that I can travel by then," he told Loretta with some gained strength in his voice.

"I believe we just might be able to do that, Edmund, if you agree to take it carefully. I'd like to be home too," she told him lovingly as they hugged.

On Sunday, Wanda and Kirk got married in a simple but touching ceremony. The genuine love felt by the two was palpable and deeply understood by everyone who was there. Loretta and Edmund gave them a gift certificate for Harrods as did Dorris and Nigel. Because of Wanda's considerable financial assets, it would have been difficult to give them actual household items.

Most other guests gave them similar gifts although a few opted for vintage wines or gourmet food baskets from Fortnum & Mason. When they returned home, the Rambars planned to send them an assortment of Chugwater Chili products from a Wyoming town of the same name.

The reception was extremely happy with warm sunny weather, the festivities passing quickly. Rambar became the sole raconteur of the evening though he was respectfully careful not to take attention away from the bride. A guest asked Kirk where they were planning for the honeymoon.

"As you're already know, we've just gotten back from two somewhat lengthy trips abroad, but I do want to show Wanda where I was born, in County Antrim in Ireland. A few months from now, we're going to be taking a proper honeymoon in Bermuda," Kirk said, smiling at his equally beaming bride.

The very next day, Edmund had an appointment with Dr. Corbett at his office.

"My medical opinion, Mr. Rambar, is that you are strong enough to travel, but with this caution: I advise that you avoid the stress of going through the two or three commercial airports before you get home. Instead, take a Medevac flight from London directly to the airport nearest your destination. You will feel much better for it and have no likely relapses in your full recovery."

"Edmund, the doctor is right, and I made sure we had travel insurance that would cover any possible circumstance of that type," Loretta assured him.

"You are truly wonderful, Loretta dear. You think of everything, and of course, we'll do it that way," Edmund replied. "In fact, it could be much more fun to have our own private plane."

On Tuesday morning, after expressing their sincere gratitude to Nigel and Dorris, their Medevac escort picked them up in a limo and took them to breakfast at a quiet restaurant en route to the airport. Wanda joined them and wished them a loving bon voyage.

Kirk, unable to get away from the MI6 offices, called and offered his regrets at not being able to see them off.

With their car having been left at the Casper airport, they opted to have their private flight land there. From London, it was an over-Canada trip much of the way but with only minor turbulence. Heading west, it seemed to only be a very long day with sunlight most of the way, unlike eastbound flights.

A light meal had been provided on the plane for them. They arrived by late afternoon and entered the terminal building. Because it was a Medevac flight, the TSA officers had been informed in advance that it would arrive at an approximate time. Edmund and Loretta were promptly cleared and walked out to their car in the small parking lot.

After some coaxing, Loretta reluctantly let Edmund drive them home. He felt exhilarated to finally be somewhat in control of his own efforts again.

Cruising along through the wide-open Wyoming landscape, their remaining stresses faded away. They were home. After the two-hour drive, they pulled up to Loretta's house. Her sister heard the vehicle approach, as did the dogs who came bounding out before the car doors could open.

"I'm so happy you both are home after all you've been through," her sister said, hugging them warmly. Princess and Hunter were more than overjoyed, yelping, licking them, and bouncing up on them, rewarded by petting and hugging all around.

"I have some coffee and cake ready," Lori, her sister, said as they walked toward the house.

"We can get our bags later," Edmund said, walking arm in arm with his wonderful wife and led by their canine companions.

The next morning, after a bountiful breakfast, which Lori insisted on preparing for them, Edmund thought that he should send a text to Larry at the CIA headquarters, letting him know they were home. It read, "Safely back home and feeling good. No more assignments please."

The phone rang a few minutes later, and the call identifier showed it was Larry. With Loretta and Edmund in tow, both dogs headed out the door for a walk. The phone rang and rang.

"Let it go. We're retired!" he told both sisters. "We are formally retired."

The end

ABOUT THE AUTHOR

Lyman L. Marfell was born in Minnesota and lived there until entering the US Army, where he served one tour in Asia. Of British/American heritage, he has traveled extensively in more than thirty countries and colonies worldwide. He is bilingual and speaks fragments of four others. His working career was in Federal law enforcement, serving in various agencies.

This author has been writing articles, short stories, advertising copy, even poetry, since high school. He first published in 1968. He lives in Wyoming with his pets and enjoys music, reading, and various hobbies. A somewhat social person, he enjoys the company of friends and staying current on world events.

CPSIA information can be obtained
at www.ICGtesting.com
Printed in the USA
BVHW040516170522
637023BV00001B/41

9 781662 468292